MW01037618

Just One Wish

Also From Carly Phillips

The Kingston Family
Book 1: Just One Night
Book 2: Just One Scandal
Book 3: Just One Chance
Book 4: Just One Spark
Book 5: Just One Wish
Book 6: Just One Dare
Book 7: Just One Kiss
Book 8: Just One Taste

Dare Nation
Dare to Resist
Dare to Tempt
Dare to Play
Dare to Stay
Dare to Tease

The Sexy Series
Book 1: More Than Sexy
Book 2: Twice As Sexy
Book 3: Better Than Sexy
Novella: Sexy Love

The Knight Brothers
Take Me Again
Take the Bride
Take Me Down
Dare Me Tonight

Rosewood Bay
Fearless
Breathe
Freed
Dream

Bodyguard Bad Boys
Rock Me
Tempt Me
His to Protect

Dare to Love Series
Dare to Love
Dare to Desire
Dare to Touch
Dare to Hold
Dare to Rock
Dare to Take

Dare NY Series (NY Dare Cousins)
Dare to Surrender
Dare to Submit
Dare to Seduce

Billionaire Bad Boys
Going Down Easy
Going Down Hard
Going Down Fast
Going In Deep

Hot Zone Series
Hot Stuff
Hot Number
Hot Item
Hot Property

Lucky Series
Lucky Charm
Lucky Streak
Lucky Break

The Simply Series
Simply Sinful
Simply Scandalous
Simply Sensual
Simply Sexy

Just One Wish

A Kingston Family Novella

By Carly Phillips

1001 DARK NIGHTS
PRESS

Just One Wish
A Kingston Family Novella
By Carly Phillips

1001 Dark Nights
Copyright 2022 Carly Phillips
ISBN: 978-1-951812-90-4

Foreword: Copyright 2014 M. J. Rose

Published by 1001 Dark Nights Press, an imprint of Evil Eye Concepts, Incorporated

All rights reserved. No part of this book may be reproduced, scanned, or distributed in any printed or electronic form without permission. Please do not participate in or encourage piracy of copyrighted materials in violation of the author's rights.

This is a work of fiction. Names, places, characters and incidents are the product of the author's imagination and are fictitious. Any resemblance to actual persons, living or dead, events or establishments is solely coincidental.

Acknowledgments from the Author

Special thanks to Nicole Andrews Moore for helping me bring Axel, Tara, and especially Bella to life.

One Thousand and One Dark Nights

Once upon a time, in the future…

I was a student fascinated with stories and learning. I studied philosophy, poetry, history, the occult, and the art and science of love and magic. I had a vast library at my father's home and collected thousands of volumes of fantastic tales.

I learned all about ancient races and bygone times. About myths and legends and dreams of all people through the millennium. And the more I read the stronger my imagination grew until I discovered that I was able to travel into the stories... to actually become part of them.

I wish I could say that I listened to my teacher and respected my gift, as I ought to have. If I had, I would not be telling you this tale now.
But I was foolhardy and confused, showing off with bravery.

One afternoon, curious about the myth of the Arabian Nights, I traveled back to ancient Persia to see for myself if it was true that every day Shahryar (Persian: شهريار, "king") married a new virgin, and then sent yesterday's wife to be beheaded. It was written and I had read that by the time he met Scheherazade, the vizier's daughter, he'd killed one thousand women.

Something went wrong with my efforts. I arrived in the midst of the story and somehow exchanged places with Scheherazade – a phenomena that had never occurred before and that still to this day, I cannot explain.

Now I am trapped in that ancient past. I have taken on Scheherazade's life and the only way I can protect myself and stay alive is to do what she did to protect herself and stay alive.

Every night the King calls for me and listens as I spin tales. And when the evening ends and dawn breaks, I stop at a point that leaves him breathless and yearning for more. And so the King spares my life for one more day, so that he might hear the rest of my dark tale.

As soon as I finish a story... I begin a new one... like the one that you, dear reader, have before you now.

Chapter One

Axel Forrester adjusted his sunglasses and leaned back against a lounge chair, grateful for the first warm, summerlike day in June in the Hamptons. Xander Kingston's dog, Bella, sat by his side.

An extra pair of glasses lay on the table beside him. He picked them up and propped them over the golden retriever's eyes. "There you go, girl. That's better, isn't it?" He patted her on the head, and she stretched out on the ground, leaving the glasses in place.

He tipped his head up to the sky and closed his eyes, enjoying the heat on his face. As a California kid, his first winter in New York had been a huge adjustment. He'd moved here last summer when he'd become the drummer for the Original Kings and had spent the first couple of months bunking at the lead singer Dash Kingston's house.

Axel learned fast that the band was a tight-knit bunch, all living in Dash's home. Until a baby scare with a groupie put Dash in need of a fake girlfriend to fix his reputation, and Axel's sister, Cassidy, had played the role.

Now Cassidy and Dash were married, having wed in front of family and friends this past winter. Axel had rented a house nearby, as had Jagger, the guitar player, and Mac, the bassist. But Axel and the guys spent more time at Dash's home studio or here at Xander's than at their own places.

Xander complained about the fact that the band had followed Dash's lead, making his house their home away from home, but nobody believed Xander really considered them unwanted company. And Sasha, the famous actress Xander had married this past spring, welcomed them, as long as they knocked first.

Given the Kingston family's dysfunctional background, courtesy of their now deceased father, the fact that four of the five siblings were settled and happy gave a guy like Axel hope that he'd meet the right woman. He was sick of the rock-star lifestyle, the parties after the shows, the groupies, and the drinking. At thirty years old, he wanted a partner for life.

And if he couldn't find the right woman?

He opened his eyes and glanced down at the dog that didn't belong to him, giving her a long rub down her spine. "We all know the truth. You're my girl, Bella, right?"

She lifted her head at the sound of her name.

"Quit trying to steal my dog's loyalty." Xander walked out of his house and joined him on the lounge chair beside him. "Why is she wearing my sunglasses?" he asked.

Axel figured the answer was obvious. "Because it's sunny out and I'm protecting her eyes."

"Know where she wouldn't be squinting? Inside. Because when I'm not home, that's where she belongs."

Xander gestured toward the house, and Axel shrugged. "Sasha let me in and said I could relax by the pool, and you know Bella loves being with me."

Xander rolled his eyes. "When you finally buy a house, make sure you have your own pool, okay?"

Axel ignored him much as Xander's brother, Dash, would have done and picked up his phone. Out of habit, he began scrolling through his social media. He had a fan page on both Instagram and Facebook that he paid someone to run and post fan-engaging photos. But if a comment struck him, occasionally Axel would answer. Otherwise, he left it to the professionals.

He also had a private page from his teenage days that only friends, family, and old acquaintances could see. He didn't often check out what the people he'd known in the past were up to, and he didn't need social media to tell him what his sister and friends were doing. But he was feeling nostalgic, so he began to scroll through the friend page for the first time in ages.

Familiar faces were displayed in his timeline. Men he'd known now had wives and kids, had just gotten engaged or married, or showed off newborns in their arms. It stood out how different Axel's life was from theirs.

One other thing stood out to him. "Jesus, these guys haven't aged well."

"What the hell are you looking at?" Xander asked.

He glanced at his friend. "Facebook. Guys I went to high school with. Half of them are bald, and the other half have huge stomachs." He shook his head and continued to scroll through the page. "The women look good," he said more to himself than to Xander. "Do you ever go through yours? It's like a blast from the past."

Xander shook his head. "No. Not a people person," he pointedly said.

Axel chuckled and didn't take offense. Annoying Xander was like the band's favorite pastime.

Another swipe of his thumb and a familiar brunette caught his gaze. He paused. Gorgeous chocolate-brown eyes stared at him, eyes he remembered looking into his as he'd eased himself inside her. She hadn't been his first, but once he'd asked her out, she'd been his only.

He blinked and continued to study her. Her face had filled out, but she was just as beautiful now as she was over ten years ago. More so, even. Dark brown hair flowed over her shoulders, and a white fluffy dog that looked like a Samoyed licked her cheek as she grinned for the photo. There couldn't be a more perfect picture to capture the essence of Tara Stillman.

"Damn," he said, making the screen larger so he could get a better look.

"What now?" Xander asked.

"Old high school girlfriend," Axel said, not really focusing on Xander. Not when memories of her came flooding back, all of them good.

He and Tara had been together from freshman to senior year of high school, and though they'd been in love – or as close to in love as teenagers could be — they'd always known their relationship had an end date. Music had always pulled at him, and as soon as he graduated, Axel had known he'd be off to audition with bands, travel to gigs, and try and make it big.

She, on the other hand, had intended to become a vet, and from the information on her Facebook page, she'd accomplished her goal. They both had, he mused, staring at the light smattering of freckles on the bridge of her nose. She'd wanted to follow in her father's footsteps and take over his veterinary practice outside of Los Angeles, near Brentwood. Obviously that part of her plan had changed, and he wondered why.

The good news, at least for him, was that she now lived on the East Coast. Was that a coincidence or a sign? Taking it as the latter, he knew he had to see her.

Axel wasn't sure how to approach a woman he hadn't kept in touch with since they'd said goodbye over a decade ago, and he wracked his brain, trying to come up with a plan.

A car horn honked in the distance, disturbing Bella, who jumped up and started to bark, causing the sunglasses to fall to the ground. Axel retrieved them and held them in his hand. After a minute, Bella settled with a low growl. *Dogs*, he thought, amused.

That was it. Dogs. He turned to Xander and asked, "Can I borrow Bella?"

"What for?" Xander asked as he shifted toward him.

Axel didn't reply because he knew how the other man would react to him borrowing the dog to visit his ex-girlfriend.

"Whatever it's for, you do realize could get your own dog, right?" Xander asked.

"Nah. Not practical while I'm renting. Besides, I'm on the road too often to commit to ownership," he said, one hand stroking the dog's fur.

"And yet you spend a remarkable amount of time at my house. Funny how that works." Xander shook his head, a grin he'd never admit to on his face.

Axel ignored the dig about the hours he hung out here. Who wanted to be alone twenty-four seven? Give it some time, and Dash or one of the other guys would show up. And if not them, Cassidy would come to see Sasha, and Axel enjoyed hanging out with the women.

As for the dog, she was the primary part of his plan to see Tara, and he wasn't about to give up. "So can I borrow Bella for a couple of hours?"

"Why do you want to borrow our dog?" Sasha had been walking on the deck, already close to the lounge chairs, when he'd asked again. She sat down on the edge of Xander's chair and placed a hand on his leg.

Xander glanced at his wife, his expression softening as he took her in, then turned back to Axel, gaze narrowed. "Wait a minute. You were just on Facebook looking up an old girlfriend. Don't tell me you want use Bella to pick up chicks."

"Chick," Axel said, correcting him because it was important. "One chick." He hoped the clarification would help the cause.

"Which chick?" Sasha asked, her eyes lighting up at his explanation.

She'd been trying to set him up with a *nice girl* for months now. But as much as he wanted to find someone, the notion of first dates and getting-to-know-you time turned his stomach. He'd just about decided he'd have to accept the inevitable and give in to Sasha's matchmaking when he'd been given a reprieve.

Now Tara was firmly in his mind.

He glanced at the phone, which had turned itself off, and reopened the screen for a look at her personal information. He was relieved there was no relationship status listed under her name and took that as another positive sign.

"Aah. Silence," Sasha said in an amused tone.

She was right. Axel wasn't eager to reveal the name of his old girlfriend, which was odd. He normally explained everything going on in his life to these people who, in a short time, had become more like family than friends.

"He's clammed up," Xander agreed, his gaze steady on Sasha as they talked over Axel, no doubt hoping he'd get annoyed and reveal more.

"That tells me the woman in question means something to him." Sasha curled one tanned leg beneath her.

Axel had had enough. "I'm right here while you're talking about me," he reminded them. Jesus fuck, these two meant business. Wasn't it enough they knew borrowing Bella was important to him?

Sasha laughed and rubbed Bella's soft head. "Just have her home by seven. She has an early curfew."

With her permission to take the dog, the muscles in Axel's shoulders eased. They'd just given him the reason he needed in order to pay Tara an impromptu visit. And that's all he'd been waiting for.

He sat up and put the sunglasses back on Bella's face. "Come on, girl. We need to make a good impression." He rose, and as if she were his pet, Bella stood and began to follow him toward the house.

Xander and Sasha stood and joined his trek inside. Once in the kitchen, Sasha handed him Bella's leash, and he hooked it to her collar, adjusting her sunglasses, which were going to be a pain in the ass to keep on. But she looked cute, and that was what mattered.

"Thanks, guys. I owe you one." His car was parked on the driveway out front, and he started to walk out of the room.

"Hey!" Xander called out.

Axel turned.

"Aren't you forgetting something?"

He narrowed his gaze. "Keys and wallet," he said, patting his pocket. "Dog, leash… Nope. I'm good."

"She's still wearing my sunglasses," Xander said, as if Axel needed a reminder.

"It's sunny out, and I have my convertible. She's going to need them."

Sasha let out an unladylike snort of laughter, causing Axel to grin, while her husband frowned and shook his head. Sometimes Axel wondered how Dash and this more serious man were related.

"Wish me luck," he said and took his companion out of the house and led her to his brand-new Chevy Corvette, in what the dealer called Elkhart Lake Blue Metallic. To Axel it was his royal blue metallic baby.

He settled Bella in the passenger seat, once again picking up the glasses she'd knocked off and adjusting them on her face.

After he turned on the engine, he opened his phone's map app, put in the business name, and started the directions.

He drove out of the circular driveway, his stomach in knots because, other than the dog beside him, he had no real plan. A short while later, he pulled up to a white clapboard building that, if not for the driveway and parking lot out front, looked more like a house than a clinic.

He cut the engine and turned to his panting passenger. "Now remember, it's been a long time since I've seen Tara, and I'm counting on you to break the ice for me."

Drool hung from Bella's mouth and Axel groaned. "Don't be

nervous. Tara was great when we were younger. In fact, she was really important to me." And he was hoping he could get to know her again and see if the old spark between them remained. "I'm sure she's got gentle hands and is a good vet. You're going to like her a lot."

He continued to talk to Bella, giving the dog a pep talk that was meant more for himself than for her. Which was ridiculous considering he was a rock star who could get any woman he desired with a simple look, cock of his head, or lifting of his lips in his signature smirk.

The fact that he hadn't been with a woman in over six months said something about his state of mind when it came to the opposite sex. No one had interested him in a long time. Until now. That he sat in his car outside a small-town vet's office like a nervous teen was pretty fucking pathetic.

But seeing Tara's photo had stirred all sorts of memories of the time they'd spent together, the fun they'd had, and the feelings they'd shared. Axel wasn't stupid and knew he only had one second chance with the woman he'd once wished he could spend the rest of his life with. And he was counting on a dog to do the heavy lifting.

Chapter Two

Dr. Tara Stillman walked out from the back area of her veterinary practice, East Hampton Vets. She'd finished an annual exam on an overweight Pomeranian named Hazel and had gone into the back area to check in on the overnighters. All her patients were doing well.

She joined her mother out front and placed a folder on the desk. "That's it until after lunch," she said. "Did you get Mrs. Frankel checked out okay?" she asked of her last patient.

Her mom nodded. "She wasn't happy with the diet you put Hazel on. She complained about the cost and said we were just trying to make money off our clients."

Tara sighed. "Hazel is seventeen pounds. The breed standard is three to seven. Even if she was a throwback to the older Poms who weighed up to fifteen, which she's not, she's still overweight. It's not good for her heart or other organs."

"All of which I'm sure you told Mrs. Frankel. If Anna would stop feeding the dog table scraps, she could have avoided needing to spend money on a special diet."

Tara nodded. "That is the truth." She smiled at her mother, who was a beautiful woman.

They shared the same thick brown hair that Tara wore past her shoulders and her mom had cut just above hers. Marsha Davidson, not Stillman anymore since she'd married Glenn Davidson, had gorgeous skin she took good care of with expensive creams and always wore her makeup perfect. She was warm and generous to a fault.

She loved to work whether it was necessary or not, a trait Tara had inherited. Marsha had been the receptionist at her first husband's and Tara's dad's veterinary clinic in California. Gary Stillman had passed away from a heart attack right before Tara had been due to leave for college, leaving Tara and her mother devastated.

Ultimately, her mom had sold the practice that Tara was supposed to join when she'd graduated vet school. Unable to bear the painful memories and wanting to be near Tara, who'd gone to her dad's alma mater in Manhattan, her mom had moved to New York City, too.

Once Marsha had adjusted to her new surroundings and being a widow, she'd moved to the Hamptons full-time and taken a job with Tara's godfather, her dad's college best friend and a veterinarian, Dr. Harry James.

Harry had become Tara's mentor. He owned this clinic and had been there for her, helping her make vet school choices, giving her a job when she graduated, and they had an agreement. When Harry was ready to retire, Tara would buy out the clinic with the money she'd been left in trust from her mother's sale of her father's vet business. Her dad had left her mom well cared for with life insurance, and her mother insisted her father would have wanted Tara to use the money to open her own practice.

Losing her father had altered the course of Tara's entire life and led to her moving across the country to settle in New York. Her mom had married Glenn Davidson, a man who treated Tara like a daughter, and she cared for him deeply. Thanks to Glenn, Tara had two stepsiblings, Amy and Connor. But being a part of the family had always made her feel disloyal to her real father. Only here, with her dog, and at the shelter where she volunteered, did Tara feel truly at home.

"Well, that's something you don't see every day," her mom said. While Tara had been lost in thought, her mom had walked to the windows looking over the parking lot.

"What is it?"

"A dog in a convertible wearing sunglasses," her mom said, laughing. "Come look!"

Tara strode over and glanced out the window, recognizing the golden dog. "Is that Bella?" she asked, narrowing her gaze. "That definitely looks like Bella Kingston. Is she on the schedule today?" Tara hadn't seen the retriever on the list of appointments, but Sasha or Xander could have called to bring her in if the dog was sick.

"No, she's not," her mom said.

A man climbed out of the Corvette, a gorgeous royal blue convertible, and strode around to get the dog from the passenger seat.

"That's definitely Bella, but that guy is not Xander."

The man in question tried and failed to keep the sunglasses on the dog's face and finally tossed them onto the seat. Tara couldn't help but laugh. People and dogs were always fun to watch. This guy had a tall, lean frame and dark brown hair. Something about him seemed familiar, but she couldn't place him. He grasped the leash and led the dog on a walk, obviously doing the smart thing before bringing the pup inside.

But before he'd walked away, he'd turned toward the building long enough for Tara to get a good look at his face. Even with aviators on his eyes, she *knew*.

"Oh, my God. It's Axel," she said, her stomach feeling like a kaleidoscope of butterflies had taken flight.

"*Your* Axel?" Her mother's voice rose in excitement.

"He hasn't been my Axel in forever." Tara covered her churning belly with her hands.

"He's the last guy you dated, so sue me for calling him yours."

Tara frowned and glanced at her mom. "I wouldn't go that far."

"Well, I would."

Tara sighed at her mother's persistence. "I don't tell you everything." Not that there was anything to tell, which was why her mother's dig hit home.

Marsha meant well and wanted her daughter happily settled, but Tara had never met a man who lived up to … well, Axel and what they'd shared. But it wasn't like she'd chosen between school and career or a nunnery, for God's sake.

Her mother took another glance between the horizontal blinds to get a better look.

"Cut it out," Tara muttered.

She stepped away from the window and headed back behind the counter, gesturing for her mother to follow. Which Marsha did. Tara did not want to get caught ogling the rock-star drummer. Even if he was her ex.

She bit down on her cheek, her heart pounding hard as she waited for him to walk in. Why was Axel here with Bella? Was he helping out his bandmate and friend? Though Tara made it a point not to check out gossip or celebrity sites, she couldn't live in this small town, especially one that emptied out after summer, and not know that Axel Forrester had joined Dash Kingston's band and moved here. She'd just been lucky enough not to have run into him before now.

They hadn't parted on bad terms all those years ago. They'd just both had life plans that had taken them in different directions. She'd always known they wanted different things out of life. He'd desired fame and travel while she'd planned to settle down in a vet practice and have a family one day. When he'd said goodbye, saying he hoped they'd reconnect in the future, she had known better. Now they were two very different people, and seeing him again could only be awkward.

At that moment, Harry walked out of the back area. He was a good-looking man, older, with salt-and-pepper hair and a distinguished goatee.

He glanced around the empty waiting room. "Everything okay?" he asked.

"Fine. There's a man in the parking lot who should be in any minute," Tara said.

Harry nodded. "I just finished eating. Would you like me to see him?"

Bless him, Tara thought. She was not ready to face the now famous Axel Forrester, former drummer for Caged Chaos and now the Original Kings, and the type of man who women threw their panties at.

"Sure," she said at the same time her mother spoke. "You're busy, Harry," Marsha said, stepping over to him.

"No, I have time for a break." His eyes crinkled in confusion at their contradictory replies.

"Good idea. Go take a break." Tara's mom urged him toward the back, her hands pushing at his arm.

"Mom! Cut it out." Taking control, Tara decided what to do. "Thanks for handling the next patient, Harry. I'll be in the back if you need me."

She walked through the double doors leading to the back rooms but remained close by so she could hear everything. She couldn't help but be curious.

"Marsha, are you okay?" Harry asked, concern in his voice.

"I'm fine. I just…" Her mother whispered something Tara couldn't hear.

Before she could find out what her mother was up to, the bells over the outside door rang, announcing the patient had arrived. Tara curled her hands into fists, her short nails digging into her skin as she waited.

"Good afternoon," her mother said in a chirpy, happy voice. "What can we do for you?" Obviously, her mother was pretending not to recognize him.

"I was hoping Dr. Stillman could see my dog." Axel's voice was familiar yet not, deeper and sexier than she remembered.

"*Your* dog?"

Tara peeked out in time to see Marsha lean over the counter to look at the animal in question. "Axel Forrester, are you bringing Bella Kingston in for Sasha and Xander?"

"Busted," he muttered, looking adorable. Dammit. "Mrs. Stillman, it's good to see you. You looked familiar, but I thought you lived in California, so I didn't think it could be you."

"What's with the Mrs. Stillman nonsense? It's Marsha. And my last name is Davidson now. I remarried after my husband passed away."

Glued to her place and unable to tear her gaze away, Tara watched as his eyes grew wide, his expression turning sad. "I'm sorry. I had no idea."

"Thank you. It was right after you left town. Anyway, what's wrong with Bella?"

Tara tore her gaze from his handsome, grown-up face with more defined and chiseled features and looked around the waiting room. Harry was gone. He must have slipped out the door as Axel walked in. Her mother definitely deserved an A in scheming.

Awkward or not, it was time to grow up and face him. Tara drew a deep breath and stepped through the doors into the reception area. "What *is* wrong with Bella?" she asked.

"Tara." Her name on those sexy lips turned her insides to mush.

"Hello, Axel."

They stared at each other for an uncomfortable few moments in which her mom remained shockingly quiet.

"Is Bella okay?" She broke the silence first.

"She's fine." An unexpected red flush rose to his face. "I was scrolling through Facebook, came across your picture, and realized you were only a mile away, so I…"

"You borrowed a dog as an excuse to see me?" She didn't know whether she was more flattered or shocked. But her traitorous heart skipped a beat.

"Yeah." He cleared his throat. "Now that we've discussed Bella, my icebreaker, I'll just get to the point. Would you have dinner with me?"

She blinked. He'd taken her by surprise. "I can't," she said, the words automatically coming out of her mouth. Getting to know this man could only lead to heartbreak. She knew it just by seeing him again.

"Why not? Do you have a husband? A boyfriend?" His jade-green eyes bored into hers. "Because your Facebook page didn't mention a relationship."

She was certain his persistence had helped him succeed in the hard-to-make-it-to-the-top music world. "No, no relationship. I'm just … busy."

"No, you are not," her mother said.

Tara had been aware of her mom watching them, looking back and forth like at a tennis match. "You don't know my schedule," Tara snapped.

Her mother ignored her and picked up one of Tara's business cards, then a pen, wrote something on the card, and held it out to Axel. "Here. Her address and cell phone number."

He didn't accept it, and his gaze remained steady on Tara's. "If you really don't want to go out with me, I get it. Too much time has passed, too much water under the bridge." He shrugged, but disappointment was clear in his expression and hunched shoulders.

His very real desire to see her again tugged at her, causing a heavy pain in her chest. Because she did want to have dinner with him. Catch up. Learn about his life. She just didn't want to open herself up to heartbreak.

"Actually, I do want to go out with you."

He released the tension he'd been holding and relaxed, straightening his shoulders, a wide smile on his handsome face. "Great."

She snatched the card from her mom's hand and passed it over.

Axel accepted it this time. "I'll pick you up at seven." He glanced at the dog, who had been so good while sitting at his side. "It'll just be us. Bella has a seven p.m. curfew," he said with a grin. "Come on," he said, and the dog, as if she belonged to him, followed him out.

Tara waited until the door shut behind him before turning on her mother. "What is wrong with you?" She'd never seen her mother act so pushy, so insistent … so over the top!

Marsha looked at Tara, disappointment in her gaze. "You were always such a bright girl. So smart. Yet here you are, turning down a date with the only man you've ever loved. *Why*?"

Oh, for God's sake. She did not want to have this conversation. "Because Axel and I don't make sense, that's why!"

"What doesn't? Dating? Relationships? Good sex? Giving me grandchildren?"

"Mom!" Tara was as horrified as she was grateful they were alone and nobody was in the waiting room. She had no doubt the vet techs in the back were having a field day with this entire conversation.

"What? Somebody has to tell it like it is! Now please explain to me why you and that handsome man don't make sense in that bright mind of yours?" Her mother sounded both concerned and exasperated.

Tara didn't like this talk any more than her mom did. "When you take away emotions and feelings, everything else about us has always been wrong. Geography, for starters."

"He lives in town, Tara."

"When he's in the studio and making music, maybe. Afterwards he spends eight months or more on tour. Sometimes in the US and other times around the world." And that wasn't the kind of relationship she wanted.

She wanted what she'd had growing up. A husband at home with her and their kids. A normal life. The kind she'd lost when her dad died. But she wouldn't say that to her mother. Marsha had tried so hard to blend the family, and it wasn't her fault Tara always felt separated from them all. They tried, but it was like she had this wall around herself she couldn't let them get beyond. And if she allowed herself to fall for Axel again, she feared she'd always be the outsider in his lifestyle, ultimately left behind.

"Honey, you're so afraid of being hurt and abandoned, like you were when your dad died, that you've closed yourself off completely."

Read my mind, why don't you, Tara thought. Her mom had always known her well.

Her mother put a hand on top of Tara's. "No man will ever meet whatever criteria you're holding out for, and the one you really want is back, yet you're too afraid to give him a chance."

A lump rose in Tara's throat, making her unable to speak.

"Just promise me you'll give Axel a chance?" her mother asked, her eyes damp.

Tara sighed. "Okay. Anything to get you to take a step back and let me think things through." She smiled to take away the sting of her words, and it worked.

Her mom grinned, then pulled her into a hug, happy with Tara's agreement to try. And since she'd agreed to a date with Axel, clearly she was going to do just that.

* * * *

Axel strode out of the vet offices, whistling as he walked, Bella trotting by his side.

"Good job," he said to the pup as he loaded her into the passenger seat and took his place behind the wheel. "You deserve a treat for being so perfect," he told her.

After starting up the car, he headed for the coffee shop in town, all the while thinking about his first glimpse of Tara. As a man surrounded by women whenever he traveled, he was familiar with beautiful females. Not to lump them into one category, but those he saw in the concert arena tried too hard to make themselves noticeable. Pushed up breasts, brightly colored hair, skimpy clothes, too-high heels.

Had he screwed around with them? Yeah, of course. He'd had needs. But had he ever been interested in any of them long-term? That would be a big hell no. Because none of them were real.

Tara was a breath of fresh air. She always had been. From her natural wavy hair that fell like silk over her shoulders to her nearly makeup-free face and those lips he wanted to kiss again, she was exactly what he'd been missing. Even if her mother had twisted her arm to go out with him, Axel was pleased with their first meeting in years.

After giving Bella her treat, he returned to Xander's and let himself in the side door of the pool gate and took a seat outside.

A few minutes later, the sliding glass door opened, and his host stepped outside.

"Dog returned before her curfew," Axel said, gesturing to the golden lying by his side on the grass.

"And you stayed?" Xander stepped over and glanced down at the dog. "What's on Bella's nose?"

"I got her a pup cup as a reward for being such a good girl." He lowered his hand to pet her soft head.

"So the trip was successful?"

Axel grinned. "Got a date at seven tonight." And he planned to do his best to charm Tara and get to know her again.

Xander nodded. "Good! You should go get ready." He tipped his head toward the gate he'd come through.

"Nah. I've got plenty of time." Axel straightened his legs on the lounge and settled in.

"You could just … go anyway."

"Are you throwing me out? Is that what you used to do to Dash?" Before the lead singer became involved with Cassidy and stopped coming by as often for company.

Xander opened his mouth, but before he could answer, the door to the house slid open again, and Sasha walked out, two large, cold drinks in her hands.

"Hi, guys. I thought you might want some iced tea." She handed each of them a glass. "How was your … excursion with Bella?" she asked.

"He got himself a date tonight," Xander replied.

"Really? That's great. Who is she?" Sasha asked, folding her arms across her chest.

"Umm, about that…" Dash met her gaze. "Turns out she's your vet."

"Dr. Stillman?" Xander asked.

"Tara?" Sasha asked at the same time.

Just hearing her name had him smiling. "We were together in high school, and we broke up after graduation. I went to do my thing in LA and audition with bands, and she went to college in New York."

"And she stayed," Sasha said, sitting down on the edge of his chair, her interest in their history obviously piqued.

"That wasn't her plan. She always wanted to go into her dad's practice outside LA, but I found out today he passed away not long after I left."

He sobered at the thought, knowing she'd probably been dealing with their breakup at the time of her father's death. He hadn't known. They'd agreed not to keep in touch because they knew it would be too hard.

"And you both ended up not just on the East Coast but here in East Hampton," Sasha mused. "Talk about fate."

He fucking hoped so.

Chapter Three

Tara's last appointment for the day cancelled, and she was able to leave the office early, giving herself extra time to get ready for her date with Axel. When she'd woken up this morning, she'd never expected to see her ex-boyfriend and first love stride into her office with a borrowed dog as a ruse to see her again. Never mind accepting a date with him tonight. Nerves fluttered in her stomach at the thought.

Her doorbell rang, and she walked through the small gatehouse on her mom and stepfather's property where she lived, to find her stepsister at the front door.

"Amy, hi! What are you doing here?"

Her stepsister, a strawberry blonde with a curvy body and bubbly personality, strode past her and into the house. "We have to talk, and I need to help you pick out clothes for your date tonight."

"Good God, word travels fast," Tara muttered.

"Your mom is beyond excited."

Tara closed the door. "I'm sure she is."

Her mom wanted nothing more than for Tara to settle down with a nice man. With Axel's return, that desire would be magnified. Her mother had always liked him and felt bad about his home situation, being raised by his grandma after his parents died when he was young.

"It doesn't help that you're five years younger than me and getting married soon," Tara said, laughing. Because she was happy for Amy, she truly was.

"Marsha loves you. Don't mind your mom's pushiness."

"Says you because you're not the one she's pushing," Tara muttered.

"Is it true your ex is Axel Forrester? As in Caged Chaos's and now the Original Kings' drummer?"

"Yes. That's him."

Amy's blue eyes lit up at her confirmation. "That is so cool. I can't wait to meet him."

Tara didn't tell her to slow her roll, but she thought it. She had to get through this first date. She certainly wasn't planning on family meet and greets.

"Let's go pick out clothes!" Amy grasped Tara's hand and pulled her toward her bedroom, obviously determined to be in charge. "You're still coming to my bachelorette party Saturday night, right?"

"I wouldn't miss it," Tara assured her stepsister.

Was she looking forward to hanging out with Amy's younger friends who still liked to party and drink the night away? And who'd likely hired a male stripper as the night's entertainment?

Not really. But when Marsha and Amy's dad, Glenn, married, Tara had had a difficult time feeling like a part of the family. It was Amy who'd latched on to Tara and pulled her into their new family unit. Tara would show up to the bachelorette party because she loved her stepsister.

"If you want me to help you choose an outfit for that, too, I'm happy to help," Amy said, leading the way into Tara's bedroom.

She couldn't help but laugh at Amy's enthusiasm and excitement. "Okay, you can help me choose both outfits."

Amy flopped onto the bed. "Show me what you were thinking about wearing."

Half an hour later, they'd come up with two outfits that Tara felt good in, then she caught up with her sister until Amy announced it was time for her to get home.

Once alone, Tara took a shower and shaved everywhere, not that she planned on exposing herself to Axel tonight, but better safe than sorry. She applied some makeup, including a light coat of foundation, blush, mascara, and a peachy-pink lip gloss, and she used her beach waver to curl her hair.

Keeping it casual, she put on the outfit she and Amy had chosen. Her favorite pair of skinny jeans and a not-quite-sheer light pink off-the-shoulder blouse, held up with slender, halter-like straps. The top had a breezy feel Tara loved. She zipped on a pearl-colored pair of chunky-heeled booties, paired them with a black lightweight faux-leather motorcycle jacket, and added some jewelry.

She set her quilted cross-body bag by the front door before heading to the kitchen to pour herself a glass of wine to calm her nerves.

Then she settled in to wait for Axel.

* * * *

Axel picked up Tara up at the address her mom had written down, which turned out to be a guesthouse with a private driveway on the property of another large estate home. He pulled his Corvette into the driveway and parked, drawing a deep breath before climbing out. He was nervous but amped up, like before a concert.

Reminding himself he had experience with pre-show anxiety, he shook it off as he normally would and strode up the cobblestone walk.

Before he could knock or ring the bell, the door opened, and Tara stood in the doorway. What would be a casual pair of jeans and top on anyone else looked gorgeous on her. Her skin tone blended well with the pink color of her blouse, and the simplicity of her silver necklace and the bracelet on her wrist made sure *she* stood out and not her accessories. She didn't deliberately reveal her cleavage like the groupies did. Instead, everything about her was genuine and called to him on a soul-deep level.

"Hi," she said, her voice a touch breathless.

"Hi, yourself. I see you're ready."

She nodded. "No sense in wasting time." She pulled the door closed and locked it behind her.

So he wasn't going to see the inside of her place before their date, and if he had to guess, she had no plans to allow him entry after. He'd just have to do his best to get her to warm up to him.

"Besides, Dakota will jump and get her white hair all over you," she said as she placed her keys into her purse.

"The Samoyed in your Facebook picture?"

She nodded. "She's my baby."

He laughed. "A fifty-pound baby?"

"Women don't discuss their weight," she said, her sexy lips lifting in a grin.

He couldn't tear his gaze from her face. "You look beautiful."

A flush stained her cheeks. "Thank you."

Reaching out, he tangled a finger in one of her long curls, causing her to draw in a shocked breath, as if he'd touched her skin.

"Do you want me to pull up the convertible top?" He tilted his head toward the car in the driveway. Women and their hair. He knew from his sister, an open top was hit or miss. He never knew what Cassidy would say when he picked her up in the 'Vette.

Tara wrinkled her nose in thought. "I did my hair but … I love the wind. I'll survive," she said with a smile.

"Down it is."

Thanks to the breeze as they drove, there wasn't much in the way of deep conversation, and he saved that for their dinner. It was early in the Hamptons summer season, and he chose a restaurant with a view of the water. At sunset it was still cool at night, especially on the water, so they took a table inside.

Axel waited until they were seated, they'd ordered and were served a bottle of Chardonnay, and the waiter had disappeared for a while, leaving them alone, to start a conversation.

"Is this where you usually go on a date?" Tara asked, beating him to the first question of the evening.

He couldn't stop his grin from forming. "Well, my last date ended with a pup cup so…"

She laughed, breaking the tension between them.

Her hand was on the table, and he reached out, placing his palm over her soft skin. Her gaze darted to their now joined hands, but she didn't break their connection.

"I gotta tell you, I haven't been on a real date since moving east."

Her eyes widened. "When was that?"

He thought back. "Right before last summer, so it's been about a year. I flew out to talk to Dash Kingston after Caged Chaos imploded, and I liked him. I hit it off with the other guys in the band. Cassidy was already living here, and I thought moving to New York would be a good change of pace."

"And do you like it here?" With her free hand, she picked up her wine and took a long sip.

"It can get a little quiet and lonely in the winter," he said honestly. "But I'm getting used to it. Dash and Xander have apartments in the city, and I was thinking that's not a bad idea." He shrugged, knowing he was still undecided. About a lot of things. "I guess I need to figure out where I want to live. I'm renting right now, and since the band is here permanently, I need to buy something for when we're not on the road."

She slid her hand from beneath his and looked away, taking him off guard. Hmm. He'd have to figure out her reaction later.

Meanwhile… "You've done a nice job keeping the conversation about me, but I asked you out to learn more about the woman you are now."

She squirmed in her seat, looking relieved when the waiter walked over.

"Have you folks decided?" he asked.

Axel shook his head. "We haven't looked at the menu. Can you give us a few more minutes?"

"Of course." The man strode over to another table, and Axel turned his focus back to Tara.

"Tell me about your time on the road," she said before he'd had a chance to gather his thoughts.

He blinked. "Okay." She obviously needed to hear about his life, so he dove in. "I guess I should start at the beginning. I left our small town and moved to LA with the band I played with throughout high school."

He took a drink of wine, which wasn't his thing, but first impressions were everything, so he'd ordered for Tara and opted to share the bottle.

She studied him, her gaze on his as she took a sip from her glass, obviously waiting to hear more.

"A guy I knew from some gigs I'd done let me crash on his couch while we performed in small bars at night. I waited tables during the day to make money to cover rent and the basics." He shrugged. "Eventually it paid off, and the Caged Chaos guys heard us play."

"That's what you'd been waiting for," she murmured.

He nodded. "The band I'd been playing with was rocky at best. The guys weren't serious about a future in music, so when Caged Chaos offered me a spot, I jumped at it."

"I wish I'd been there to celebrate with you," she said with a smile that lit up her eyes. "I'm so happy you achieved your dream, though I'm not surprised. Not with how talented you are."

He grinned. "I always was good with my hands."

She rolled her eyes and laughed.

"Okay, your turn. How did you get to where you are today?" He saw the moment her expression changed, her smile dimmed, and the sparkle in her eyes went out.

He wished he hadn't asked, but if he wanted to get to know her again, he needed to hear everything, including learning what happened after her dad passed away.

Chapter Four

Tara hated talking about that time in her life when everything had fallen apart. But she was sitting across the table from the man who had once known her better than anyone, who'd heard all her hopes, her dreams, and her future plans. He deserved to know.

She rested her elbows on the table and leaned forward. "I was planning to go to college. Mom and I were buying all the necessities when Dad died of a heart attack." She swallowed over the painful lump in her throat, one that never failed to go away, even over a decade later. His receptionist had found him on the floor in the back room of his practice, already gone.

"I wanted to stay home with Mom, go to school in California or take a year off, but she refused to let me do either. She knew how much I wanted to become a vet and work with my dad." She drew in a deep breath. "So I went to college in New York, and Mom handled his estate. When I came home at the end of my first year, she told me she didn't want to stay in California. That she was too lonely."

"So what happened?" His gentle voice washed over her, giving her strength.

"Mom moved to New York to be closer to me, and I continued on with veterinary school in the city. And my dad's best friend from his time in school, my godfather, owned a practice that had offices in Manhattan and East Hampton. I worked with him during summers and on breaks, and he took me in when I graduated." She smiled at the memory of how generous Harry had been from the day she'd relocated to the city.

"I like seeing that smile," Axel said.

She lifted one shoulder. The pain would always be there, but she'd found things to smile about, too. "I guess good did come out of the bad. Mom met her new husband, I got stepsiblings out of the deal, and I'll eventually buy Harry's practice when he retires." She paused. "Mom set up a trust fund for me after selling Dad's practice."

Axel nodded in understanding.

"It's just that Dad and I were so close, and I still miss him," she admitted.

He took her hand again and cupped it in his own. "I know. You were a daddy's girl."

She'd bet none of his groupies ever saw that soft smile, and warmth slid through her veins. "Yeah. I guess I was."

"But despite the setbacks, you achieved your dream, too. Maybe it's different than you imagined it would be, but you're a vet, and that's something to be proud of." His thumb brushed back and forth over the top of her hand. "I'm proud of you."

She hated to admit how good it felt for him to offer her comfort. To have him here. When she knew better than to put any hopes in a transient man who traveled the world with his band, who didn't own his own home, and who might want an apartment in Manhattan, a place she rarely ventured anymore.

They definitely had lingering feelings for each other. And just watching him grin, his eyes crinkled with laughter. The simplest of touches aroused her in ways no man ever had. But their basic differences, the reasons they'd split up in the first place, hadn't changed.

She wanted a stable life, a home, and eventually a husband and a family with her pets. So far, nothing he'd said indicated he desired the same.

The waiter returned and they glanced at their menus, each ordering dinner. The meal passed quickly and comfortably — if she excluded the sexual tension simmering between them. The lingering glances, his gaze focusing on the way she slid her tongue over her bottom lip to capture the last of her wine, and how she couldn't stop staring at his handsome face and memorizing the differences between the teenager and the man.

After dinner was finished and he paid the bill, they walked out of the restaurant. Surprisingly, the temperature hadn't dropped, and it was still pleasant outside.

"Do you want to take a walk on the beach?" he asked, obviously not ready to take her home.

She'd had such a nice, relaxing time with him, but a walk on the beach had romantic overtones, and she knew it would be a mistake to say yes. They'd gotten reacquainted, and it was time to end the evening.

"I would, but I have to be up early for work in the morning. I operate on Wednesdays." Though true, she recognized the excuse for what it was and had no doubt he did, too.

He studied her face, and whatever he saw there had him nodding. "Next time, then."

She wanted to object to the notion of another date, but Axel had already turned and handed his ticket to the valet. When the car arrived, the valet helped her into the front seat, and they drove home in silence, her hair whipping in the wind.

Axel reached over and took her hand in his, threading their fingers together. He was nothing if not determined, something she ought to know from how he'd made it to the top of his chosen profession. Not an easy feat.

Instead of fighting him, she closed her eyes and allowed herself to enjoy his touch, the glide of his finger over her hand, and the sound of his voice as he sang along with the classic rock song on the radio.

He walked her to her front door and paused. Nerves fluttered in her belly as she waited for him to kiss her. After all, it wasn't a typical first date, not when they already knew each other so well. Intimately, in fact. Which meant maybe he expected more than a kiss. If he wanted to come inside and end up in her bed, she wasn't ready.

And if she let him in, she was afraid she wouldn't be able to turn him down. Which meant she'd have to do it here on the porch. Nerves churning, uncertainty about her choice settled inside her, but sending him away would be for the best.

She put the key in the door and turned the lock but left it closed so Dakota wouldn't come running out.

Turning slightly, she faced him. "Thanks for tonight. It was great seeing you again."

A slight smile lifted his lips and he stepped closer.

His cologne, a musky aftershave that was new to her but suited him, wafted around her. She liked the scent and wanted to breathe it in deeper. Breathe him in. Despite all the mental warnings she'd given herself on the drive home, desire for him pounded inside her.

"You make that sound like goodbye, Tara." He leaned in, his face close to hers. "It's not. In fact, you'll be seeing me again soon." He pressed a kiss to the tip of her nose and stepped back. "Now let me watch you get inside safely before I take off."

She blinked in surprise. He hadn't asked to come in or requested anything more than she'd been willing to give. She stared at him a beat too long before turning the knob and letting herself inside, using her knees to keep Dakota from bolting out to greet him.

She shut the door, leaned back against it, and blew out a deep breath, her heart pounding hard in her chest. All that anticipation and worry for nothing. And though she hated to admit it, even to herself, she was beyond disappointed he hadn't even tried for a good-night kiss.

* * * *

With a hard-on and no outlet other than his hand available, Axel walked into his house and flicked on the lights. Fucking place was too big and too lonely. After living at Dash's with the guys last summer, he'd never adjusted to being by himself. Even in LA, he'd shared an oversized apartment with one of his Caged Chaos bandmates. And since he didn't know where his home base would be, he hadn't ordered furniture, which meant he was living in a place that was empty and echoed.

He tossed his keys onto the kitchen counter and grabbed a beer from the fridge. Yeah, he'd had a good time with Tara tonight. The only thing that could make it better would have been ending up in her bed, but he'd known going in he had a long road ahead. One he'd have to take slowly. Winning her trust wasn't going to be easy.

There was something about him or his life that bugged her, and he wasn't sure what. Yet. He drank half the beer and poured the rest down the drain before heading into his room. After stripping and climbing into bed, he replayed the few minutes by her door at the end of the night.

He'd leaned in close, inhaling her warm, vanilla scent, and his dick grew hard. Fighting the need to kiss her lips and take possession of her luscious mouth hadn't been easy, but this was a marathon, not a sprint.

And he was adult enough not to listen to his cock and to think with his brain, because she'd be worth it in the end. When he'd stepped back and glanced at her face, a flash of disappointment had flickered in her gaze. At least he hoped that was what he'd seen.

On that note, he grabbed his dick in his hand, pictured Tara's mouth wrapped around him, and took care of the hard problem that would have kept him awake.

* * * *

The next morning, the band planned to work on a new song, and Axel drove over to Dash's house to meet up with the guys. His sister had long since given up her job as their assistant, and her replacement, a preppy guy named Brent, was perfect for the position. He kept them well fed, hydrated, and managed each of their appointments and the band's schedule as a whole.

Since firing their manager, Dean Jerome, last summer, all four band members had spent hours discussing what they wanted for the future. Instead of someone to negotiate all their business, they'd hired a music lawyer to handle contracts, and the rest of their operations were done in house by separate people. No one person would take a percentage and fuck with them ever again.

Though Axel had been new to the band when Dean started pushing too hard and acting outside of the band's best interests, the man had an issue with Cassidy as Dash's girlfriend. If Dash hadn't stepped up first, Axel might have pummeled Dean into the ground for the way he'd treated Cass. But Dean was long gone, and Brent did a good job juggling the various people who needed access to the band.

The four band members spent the day jamming the song, rewriting the chorus, and arguing over key. All normal in a day's work. Afterwards, Jagger and Mac went to grab dinner, and Axel joined them. Otherwise he'd be doubly tempted to call or text Tara. He didn't want to play games, and the urge to ask her out again was strong.

He figured she needed a day or two to process their date, seeing him again, and of course, time to build up her walls. He expected it. Just as he planned to knock them down.

Friday morning, he caved, and after he parked in Dash's huge driveaway, he called her before heading inside.

"Hello?" Tara answered in a breathless voice that reminded him of a hot, sweaty session in bed.

"Did I catch you at a bad time?" he asked.

"I'm just running late this morning. I overslept, which isn't like me," she said, her voice still husky.

He adjusted his dick in his pants. "I want to take you out Saturday night." He got to the point, not wanting to keep her long if she was busy.

"I'm… Saturday's not good. I have plans."

His stomach plummeted at her words. Before he could ask what those plans were and with whom, because yeah, he wanted to know, she spoke but obviously not to him.

"Oh, hi, Mom. Sorry I'm late," she said.

"Your first patient is already in one of the rooms," he heard her mother say.

Shit.

"I have to go, Axel. I'm sorry," she said and disconnected the call, leaving him holding the phone in his hand.

He understood she had a job to do, so her hanging up didn't bother him. Turning him down on Saturday night for what he figured was a date – because what else would a smart, beautiful woman have planned on the weekend? – that stung.

* * * *

Tara's first appointment of the morning was a quick one, a beagle named Buster with bad breath. They scheduled him for a teeth cleaning, and he was on his way. Her second patient was running late, and considering Tara's own harried morning, she couldn't be upset.

She walked over to her mom, who sat at the reception desk, confirming appointments for later in the week. Her mother took one look at her and put down the receiver.

"Did you really tell Axel you couldn't go out with him because you had plans?" Disappointment lit her mother's gaze.

Tara should have known her mother was eavesdropping on her call as she'd rushed in earlier. "I did because I do. It's Amy's bachelorette party, remember?" She looked over her mom's shoulder at the rest of today's schedule.

Her mom let out an exaggerated sigh. "Where, oh, where did I go wrong with you? The man probably thinks you have a date!"

Tara blinked. "I didn't mean to make him think that. I was just rushing into work." And if he had assumed her being busy meant another man had asked her out? It wasn't like they were exclusive or even officially dating.

"What would you have said if you weren't in a rush and didn't have Amy's party?" her mom asked.

"I'm not sure," Tara said. Nor was she going to get into the discussion with her mother.

She'd already spent the days since their date obsessing over every word she'd said, he'd said, and his lack of a kiss afterward. But mostly she'd thought about his present circumstances. He rented a house, traveled for tours, and was the furthest thing from settled she could imagine.

"I'm starting to think you don't ever want to get married," her mother said on a huff just as the phone rang, saving Tara from further conversation.

And since her next patient walked through the door, she was spared from overthinking as well.

Chapter Five

Halfway into the bachelorette party, Tara regretted attending. The first part of the night was a dinner to which Tara's mom and her sister, Tara's aunt Jeanne, along with Amy's mother, Barbara, and her future mother-in-law, Liza, had been invited. Amy and her friends were young enough that, though Tara liked them, she had few interests in common with them.

She'd ended up sandwiched between the older adults. They'd eaten dinner and were on to dessert. Afterwards, the bridesmaids, Tara included, were going to head to the bar on the other side of the restaurant for the more fun part of the evening. At least according to Amy and her friends.

Dessert was served, and Tara was on her second glass of wine.

"Are you dating anyone, Tara?" It didn't matter who asked. The bomb had been dropped.

Before she could reply, her mother answered. "Her first love is back in town. Isn't rekindling an old flame romantic?"

"Mom, that's not true." She gestured to the nearest server and smiled when she walked over. "Can I please get a Long Island Iced Tea?" she asked, ready for something stronger to drink.

"Of course," the young redhead said.

Tara glanced around her end of the table. Her mother was talking about Axel and how famous he was now and his history with both bands. Marsha had done her research.

"Make it strong, please," she said quietly.

The server laughed and nodded before heading off to the bar.

"Mom, Axel is an old boyfriend. Nothing more," she said, smiling at the other women so she didn't sound like she was scolding her mom.

"Oh, Tara. Amy's five years younger than you, and *she's* getting married." Aunt Jeanne wagged her finger at Tara. "You're not getting any younger, you know."

Before Tara could reply, one of Amy's bridesmaids, whose name Tara couldn't remember, stood up and clapped her hands to get everyone's attention. "Game time!"

Tara breathed a sigh of relief at the interruption that would save her from being harassed by her mom and aunt.

"Whenever someone says the word *baby*, we all have to do a shot!" Amy said, lifting her glass and grinning at Tara. Apparently she'd overheard the conversation and knew a good way to get drunk when she heard one.

"It's not a baby shower," she reminded her sister, but Amy wouldn't meet her gaze.

A man placed shots of what Tara assumed was vodka in front of each person at the table, and the other girls clapped their hands and squealed in excitement.

Let the fun begin, Tara thought, laughing. At least she hadn't taken her car and had come with her mother. Once Marsha left, Tara would call an Uber to get home later.

"Tara, your mom isn't getting younger, either, and I know she wants grand*babies*," Aunt Jeanne said loudly.

So much for changing the subject. Tara looked at her aunt, who not-so-innocently grinned. The woman clearly knew what she was doing.

"She said *babies*! Shot!" someone called out.

Only too happy to oblige, Tara picked up the little glass, braced herself because it had been years since she'd done one, and poured the liquor into her mouth and gulped it down. The alcohol burned as it slid past her throat and into her chest. No sooner had she swallowed than the empty glass had been replaced with a full one.

Her aunt, mom, and the other women were on a roll, with Tara in their sights. Ribbing her about her single status and failure to provide her mother with a grandbaby amused the older women, who should have gone home by now. *They* weren't doing shots, Tara noticed, but she played the game, getting drunk in an effort to tune out the fun around her.

By the time her mother was ready to go, offering Tara a ride before she left, Tara was feeling no pain. She was even enjoying the bridesmaids, who'd taken over the baby challenge, using it against each other. She promised her mother she'd call a car and assured her she'd get home fine.

A while later, the room began to spin, and Tara stopped drinking. She'd already fended off one or two men who wanted to buy her more alcohol, and she pulled out her phone since she hadn't checked it all evening. Her texts and emails were empty, and she started thinking about Axel.

She'd done her best to put him out of her mind because they were so mismatched. But sitting at a table alone, Amy and her friends dancing on the small designated area, she couldn't help but pull up his number.

The desire to text him was strong, and a war began to wage inside her mind.

Angel Tara: *Don't do it, you're drunk.*

Devil Tara: *He asked you out. He'd love to hear from you.*

Angel Tara: *Getting further involved with him can only lead to hurt and trouble.*

Devil Tara: *Don't be a* baby.

Tara didn't miss the irony of that particular word. It had gotten her drunk and to this point in the night, phone in hand. And if they hadn't broken up all those years ago, maybe she'd be married with his baby, and she wouldn't have been the subject of her aunt and mother's pushing and prodding.

Devil Tara spoke up again: *Do it. Do it. Do it.*

Angel Tara was suspiciously silent.

She glanced at the screen, waiting for the blurriness to subside. How many shots had she had, anyway?

She pulled up Axel's name and typed.

Tara: *Where are you?*

Her cell buzzed immediately.

Axel: *At Xander's.*

Tara: *With the babies?*

She blinked, some rational part of her brain telling her she'd regret this tomorrow, but drunk as she was, she couldn't bring herself to care.

Axel: *What babies and where are you???*

Tara: *The kids we would've had if we'd stayed together.*

She thought she'd misspelled a few words but couldn't be sure. She hit send anyway.

Axel: *WHERE ARE YOU? Did your dick of a date get you drunk?*

Tara: *Yep, I'm drunk. The phone's spinning. What date?*

Axel: *TELL ME WHERE YOU ARE?*

Tara: *Amy's bachelorette party.*

Axel: *WHERE???*

Tara leaned over in her seat and nearly toppled onto the floor. Amy, who'd just walked over, flung herself into a chair. "Why's the ceiling going in circles?"

"Ames, where are we?" Tara asked, glancing up at the direction her sister had pointed, narrowing her gaze to see if she could see circles, too.

"We're at Shenannananigans," Amy said.

Tara did her best to spell that for Axel and sent him the name of the bar.

"Amy!" Her fiancé, Kenneth, strode up to her. "Honey, are you okay?"

Tara glanced over to see her sister still staring at the ceiling. "She's drunk," Tara told him.

"So is you," Amy said.

"Yep."

Kenneth shook his head and gestured for a server to come over. "Can I get two glasses of water for the women?" he asked.

"Coming right up," the familiar redhead said.

"No water. My bladder's full." Amy clutched her stomach.

"Let's go to the ladies' room," Tara said, grabbing Amy's hand and pulling her up.

"Come right back here," Kenneth ordered. "No more alcohol."

Amy bobbed her head in response, then closed her eyes. "Bad idea."

A few minutes later, Tara had gone with her sister to the bathroom. With her bladder empty, she would be able to drink the water Kenneth had ordered. She knew she'd appreciate that tomorrow. Right now? She was still feeling beyond buzzed. In fact, she was drunk enough to know she would be hurting tomorrow.

With Amy's hand in hers, Tara attempted to walk a straight line back to Kenneth and not bump into anyone in the process. At least her future brother-in-law would take her home, because she knew enough to realize she didn't want to take an Uber alone in her drunken state.

She plopped back into the chair, Amy settled on Kenneth's lap, and he slid a glass of water toward her.

"Drink this," he said to Tara before turning to his fiancée and handing her the water, helping her drink it without spilling.

Tara downed the water and wiped her wet mouth with the sleeve of her shirt. When she looked up, it was into familiar jade-green eyes staring at her, a combination of concern and amusement visible in the depths. Along with a sexy-as-hell smile on his oh-so-kissable lips.

"Axel!" She jumped up from her seat. Happy to see him, she threw her arms around his neck. "Why are you here?"

He pried her off him but kept her hands clasped in his. "I realize drunk texting an ex is a thing, but you scared me. I thought you were on a date and something was wrong." He frowned at her, releasing his grip.

She shook her head. "No date! I'm at a bachelorette party and everyone was talking about babies. Babies made me drink. They also made me think of you." Suddenly exhausted, she fell against him.

Strong arms wrapped around her, and she knew she no longer had to worry about anything. She closed her eyes and sighed because she felt safe.

* * * *

Axel sat in the family room at Xander's house, enjoying a Kingston get-together. He had no family other than his sister, and he was grateful Dash's family made him part of theirs. Despite the good mood of the people around him, Axel couldn't shake his bad mood since Tara had turned him down for a date, and here it was, Saturday night, and he was wondering if she was with someone she had feelings for.

Melly, Dash's mother, sat down beside him. He didn't remember much about his own mother, but Melly Kingston, in the short time he'd known her, tried to fill that hole.

"You look sad and alone," she said.

He shook his head. "I'm not alone. I have Bella for company." He ran his hand over the dog's soft fur.

She eyed him the way only a mother could, indicating she wasn't buying what he was selling. "I'm here to listen," she offered.

He looked down and remained silent, thinking about whether he wanted to get into his problem.

"It's about a woman, isn't it?" Melly asked.

Axel lifted his head and met her gaze. "Yeah. My high school girlfriend. We broke up after graduation because we were going in different directions. Now she's here. In East Hampton. She's Bella's vet." He grinned at the dog who he'd used as a buffer.

"So you've reconnected?"

He nodded. "We went on one date. I asked her out again for tonight, but she said she was busy."

"I see. So you're worried she's out having fun with someone else," Melly said.

"Yeah." Among other things. "I don't want her to fall into a relationship with someone else before I get the chance to win her back." He flexed his fingers, a habit he'd developed to keep his hands limber.

"Does she know you want to get back together?" Melly asked. "Or does she think you're asking her on casual dates?"

"Umm…"

"Obviously you need to state your intentions. The woman's not a mind reader," Melly said, her wry smile making him laugh.

"I–" Before he could reply, his phone buzzed with a text message. He pulled it out of his pocket and glanced at the screen.

Tara: *Where are you?*

"Speak of the devil," he said with a grin.

Melly tipped her head. "Yes? What does your lady want while she's out on her date?"

Axel bit the inside of his cheek as he continued to text with Tara, lost at half of what was coming from her.

"She's drunk texting me," he said at last. The next few messages had him raising his eyebrows, confused, laughing, and then concerned.

"Go get her," Melly said, watching him with amusement on her face.

"She didn't ask me to do that." But she was talking about his babies. Something he couldn't explain to Dash's mother.

"Men." Melly rolled her eyes. "If a woman tells you where she is, she wants you to come get her." She placed her hands on her thighs, her manicured nails a pop of pink. "And on that note, I'm going to leave you alone to go pick her up and tell her how you really feel," she said, rising to her feet and heading over to her daughter, Chloe.

"Thanks," he called after her.

The next thing he knew, he was striding into the restaurant and bar in town. A combination of relief that there'd been no date warred with amusement at the drunk messages he'd received.

He took one look at the woman in the chair wiping her mouth with her sleeve and knew just how drunk the usually put-together, well-mannered Tara was.

For all the times he'd seen her drink at high school parties, he'd never seen her like this. Glassy-eyed, cheeks flushed, splayed back against the chair in a heap. She was still the most beautiful woman he'd ever seen.

She glanced up and met his gaze, surprise opening her eyes wide. "Axel!" She hopped up from her seat and wrapped her arms around his neck, which he had to admit felt damned good. "Why are you here?" she asked.

He needed to gauge how inebriated she was and how to deal with her, so he pulled her off him but kept her hands clasped in his. "I realize drunk texting an ex is a thing, but you scared me. I thought you were on a date and something was wrong."

He didn't realize how worried he'd been until he'd walked in and seen her safe and sound.

She shook her head, her brown hair falling around her face. "No date! I'm at a party and everyone was talking about babies. Babies made me drink. They also made me think of you," she babbled.

He released his hold on her hand as she fell into him. He caught her before she could slide to the ground and held her tight against him. She felt good in his arms, but given the reason, he wasn't going to be admitting his intentions for them tonight.

"Tara," a woman said in a singsong voice. "Who's the hunk?"

Since she was sitting on another man's lap, Axel knew it wasn't a pickup line. She was obviously drunk, too.

He shifted Tara against him. "I'm Axel. An old friend of Tara's. And you are?"

The woman stared at him through her heavy-lidded gaze. "The drummer and Tara's ex!" Her voice rose in excitement.

"This is Amy, Tara's stepsister," the man said, his amusement clear. "I'm Kenneth, Amy's fiancé."

"Nice to meet you," Axel said. Tara's head was on his shoulder, her body weight leaning against him. "Anything I need to know?"

"Other than a successful bachelorette party without strippers? Not a thing." Kenneth paused. "I was going to take them both home, but Tara seems to be settled where she is," he said, chuckling.

Axel grinned. "I've got her." Which was easier said than done, but eventually he managed to encourage Tara to lean on him as she walked to the car. The top was closed, and he leaned down to strap her in, debating about where to take her and deciding to go to his place. He knew where everything she'd need was located, and he lived closer.

Only when he carried her into the house did he realize he'd only furnished his bedroom and minimally at that, which meant she'd be sleeping in his bed tonight.

Chapter Six

Tara was too old to drink like a teenager. She woke up, her head pounding and her mouth feeling like cotton and tasting like something foul had settled in there. Her bladder was screaming at her, and she slowly pulled herself to a sitting position, waited for the waves of nausea and head throbbing to settle, before opening her dry eyes.

She looked around the unfamiliar room and panic seized her. Where was she? Who had she gone home with? Heart pounding, she glanced down to see her bare legs and a man's T-shirt covering her important parts. No bra but panties still on. Thank God. She hoped that meant she'd passed out and nothing had happened. But where and with whom?

She couldn't remember last night, and a careful look at the other side of the bed told her she was alone. She blew out a breath, stood, and made her way to the bathroom.

She found an array of towels stacked on the counter, a folded man's shirt, toothbrush in a package, and realized whoever had taken care of her seemed to be looking out for her.

She closed the door and locked herself in before brushing her teeth well, then stripping down and taking a hot shower. Although there was only generic shampoo and men's soap, she used both. Once she came out feeling fresh, she dried off, put her underwear on inside out and used the new shirt left for her. She glanced in the mirror, took in her tangled hair and the Caged Chaos logo on the shirt, and knew exactly whose house she was in.

She let out a low groan, trying her best to remember how he'd found her last night at Amy's bachelorette party. Texts. Shit. She'd drunk texted him. Where was her phone so she could see how much damage she'd done to her self-respect?

Pulling in a deep breath, she opened the bathroom door. Steam escaped as she stepped into the bedroom to find Axel sitting on what she assumed was his side of the bed.

He was barefoot, wearing a pair of faded jeans, and the button was undone. His chest had a light coating of hair, and he had muscles indicating he worked out. His abs were a six-pack any woman would drool over, and his flat stomach made her want to lick from his belly button down. Her nipples puckered beneath the T-shirt.

He caught her staring, and his lips lifted in a sexy, knowing grin. "See something you like?" he asked, amused.

Caught but refusing to admit it, she folded her arms across her chest. "How did I get here?" she asked.

"You drunk texted me, and I came to make sure you got home safely. I brought you a glass of water, some toast with jelly, and two ibuprofen." He gestured to the nightstand on the side of the bed where she'd slept.

She swallowed hard. "Thank you." She walked over to the items he'd left for her and sat down, taking her time to eat the piece of toast before taking the pills.

Feeling better, she turned to face him. She appreciated what he'd done for her, but she'd woken up in his shirt. "Axel, did you undress me?"

"I did, but let's be honest, I've seen you naked before." His eyes gleamed at her question. "But I did my best not to look. I just wanted you to be comfortable."

"And did you … did we…?"

He shook his head. "Drunk texting might be your thing, but consent is mine. I wouldn't take advantage, and you know me better than that." He sounded hurt by her question, and she saw the pain in his eyes.

She glanced down. "I didn't mean it the way it came out. I just woke up and couldn't remember much." She turned and scooted over to his side of the bed, facing him. "Don't take anything I say to heart. I'm hung over."

"What about what you said last night?"

She shook her head and regretted the motion. "I need to see my phone." Because the actual words weren't coming back to her.

He grinned at her lapse in memory. "You asked if I was home with the babies."

"What babies?" she asked, trying not to let her mortification show.

"According to you? The ones we would have had if we'd stayed together." His amusement was clear in both his tone and his expression.

Oh, now she was beginning to remember. Her mom and aunt pressuring her about not being in a relationship and wanting her to have babies. Then the shots with the bridesmaids.

"I'm so sorry about that." The memory had her cheeks heating in embarrassment.

"I'm not. It told me you think about the same things I do. All the things that could have been if we hadn't put our careers ahead of our *feelings*." Those deep green eyes held her in place while the word *feelings* reverberated between them.

"Axel, that was a long time ago. We were kids, and we had to grow up and become who we were meant to be." Even if losing him had left a hole in her heart that had never healed.

"I agree." He sat up straighter. "But here we are, on the same side of the country, in the same town, no less. Wouldn't you call that fate?"

"What about coincidence?" she asked, not ready to concede because she was so scared of losing people in her life and he had one foot out the door just by virtue of his profession and how he lived.

Before she knew it, he'd leaned forward, grabbed her hand, and pulled. She tumbled forward, falling beside him until they were face-to-face.

"Fate," he insisted before his lips captured hers. One taste and she wasn't about to pull away. She'd missed him for years, and now they were together again.

She'd take the time she could get.

She grabbed on to his hair and kissed him back, her tongue meeting his. He groaned, rolling her onto her back so he was on top and in charge. She didn't care as long as they finished what they'd started.

She'd worry about the ramifications and feelings she had for him later.

Even if later was too late.

* * * *

The second Tara's tongue slipped into his mouth, Axel had her okay and flipped her onto her back so he could devour her more thoroughly. His damned jeans were rubbing against his aching cock, but he couldn't bring himself to break their kiss long enough to undress himself yet.

He'd waited too many years to taste her again, and he wanted to savor the moment. Her fingers tangled in his hair, and she kept his head in place, their tongues tangling, teeth clashing, as a tentative, sweet moment turned into a needy frenzy.

She released his hair and slid her hands between them. He raised his upper body so her fingers could glide over his chest and work their way to his nipples, her thumbs pressing into the peaks.

He groaned and arched his hips, wanting to feel her heat against his dick and not the barrier of clothing. She must have read his mind because her hands slipped lower, and she struggled with getting the zipper over his rigid erection.

He maneuvered himself off her, slid to the edge of the bed, and rose to his feet. He'd gone commando and yanked his jeans down his legs and kicked them off. Condoms were in the nightstand, and he opened the top drawer, took one out, and tossed it beside her on the bed.

He glanced over to find Tara waiting, propped against the pillows. She'd removed the shirt she'd borrowed along with her panties, giving him a clear view of her glistening pussy.

He'd thought he was already as hard as he could get. He'd been wrong. Letting out a groan, he wrapped his fingers around himself, doing his best to hold back.

Her gaze dropped to watch, and he pumped twice. Pre-cum leaked on the head of his erection, and she sighed.

"How much longer are you going to torture me?" she asked.

Her pleading tone got to him, but he wanted to take in the view before he lost himself inside her. Her hair fell over her shoulders in tangled waves, her skin was creamy, and her body had more curves than he remembered.

She'd filled out and was every inch a woman now. *His* woman, no matter what she thought.

"You're fucking beautiful."

Her gaze raked over him, studying the tattoos on his arms and chest before meeting his eyes. "So are you. Now get over here and fuck me before I lose my mind."

He registered her choice of words and decided not to let it go. He'd fucked groupies. Not once in his past had he fucked Tara, and he wouldn't start tonight.

He placed a knee on the bed and climbed over her, leaning down and bracing his hands on either side of her head. "We need to get something straight." He paused for effect. "I'll never fuck you."

Those pretty eyes opened wide.

"Will I make love to you? Yes. Fuck you? Not without a good combination of feeling involved."

Knowing she'd argue or give him shit, he slid down her body, parted her thighs, and buried his mouth in her sex. The only sound after that was a long, low moan.

As he licked and nipped his way around her pussy, she writhed on the bed. Her hips arched, pressing herself against his mouth, and he fucking loved it, flicking his tongue and sucking her juices. He never gave oral with a one-night stand. Had it done to him? Yeah, but not in reverse. Was he a dick? Probably, but he didn't care. It was reserved for more intimate relationships. He'd had one or two, but none had lived up to Tara.

He pushed thoughts of prior experience, his and hers, out of his mind. All that mattered from today forward was them.

As he devoured her, her taste brought back the best memories of the past. But the woman with her hands in his hair and her pussy grinding against his face wasn't the same shy girl he'd known.

Thank fuck for that, he thought, and concentrated on making her come. Once he began nipping at her clit, it didn't take long for her legs to shake and the noises coming from her to deepen.

He slid one finger inside her and pumped in and out, his mouth teasing her, bringing her to a frenzy, and slowing down all over again.

"Don't stop. *Please*, don't stop."

His dick throbbed against the bedding as he added a second finger and sucked hard on her clit, flicking his tongue back and forth before pressing down with his tongue and curving his fingers inside her.

"Oh, my God. I'm almost, almost … there!" she cried out, her inner walls rippling around him, clasping his fingers in her wet heat.

He didn't let up until her orgasm subsided and she collapsed against the bed, her muscles finally lax. Satisfied he'd taken care of her, he rubbed his face against her thigh and sat up on the bed.

Her eyes remained closed as she caught her breath, and he took the time to grab the condom wrapper, rip it open, and roll it on. At the sound, she opened her eyes and watched, which only made what he was doing feel hotter, and his cock pulsed in his grip.

Dammit, he was afraid he'd come at first thrust; that's how much he wanted her. Rising, he pressed her knees back and wedged himself between her legs, his cock poised at her wet entrance.

"Look at me," he said.

Her gaze met his. He nudged his cock at her entrance, finding her so wet he slipped inside and paused, clenching his jaw and thinking of anything but how damn good she felt.

She lifted her hands, and he entwined their fingers, then thrust deep. Her hips rose to meet him as he filled her completely.

"Fuck, baby, you feel good."

She grasped his shoulders, her nails digging into his skin. "You do, too. Move, Axel. Please."

Unable to remain upright and hold back, he fell forward, his hands on either side of the mattress, supporting his weight. And then he did what she asked, pumping his hips in and out, making certain she felt him, watched him, and wasn't thinking this was just sex.

His cock experienced every clasp and release as her pussy tried to hold on to him while he pulled himself out and thrust back in.

"I missed you," he told her, "so damned much." He lowered his hips and ground himself against her until her eyes nearly rolled back in her head.

"Oh, God. Keep doing that," she said, her legs shaking on either side of him.

"Keep your eyes on me and I will."

She locked her gaze with his, and he began to move, grinding himself against her, doing his best not to let go until she let out a moan, her entire body seizing around him.

Only then did he allow himself to let go and feel everything, his climax ripping through him and pulling him under. All he could think and feel was Tara, surrounding him, holding on to him, and fulfilling him.

When he came back to himself, he realized he'd collapsed on top of her and rolled to his side, letting her breathe more easily.

He pulled off the condom and forced himself to leave the bed to get rid of it and wash up quickly before rejoining her. He propped himself up on one elbow and met her gaze. He already knew he needed to be one step ahead of her or else she'd take the time to rebuild her walls.

"We still click," he said, grinning because how could he not? She was still in his bed. He reached out and tucked her hair behind one ear.

She blew out a breath. "I can't argue with that," she murmured. "I'll be right back. I need the bathroom, too."

She stood and walked into his master bath, returning a few minutes later. "Is there bottled water in the refrigerator?"

He nodded. "I'll get it."

"No, it's fine. I'm already up." She grabbed the T-shirt she'd been wearing and put it on, covering up that gorgeous body. "Do you want one?"

"Sure. The kitchen is–"

"I'm sure I can find it unless the house is a maze." She laughed and walked out of the room, a smile on her face.

When she returned, water in hand, her expression was much more subdued. She handed him his bottle, put hers on the nightstand, and climbed back into bed. Without taking her shirt off again.

"What's wrong?" he asked.

She picked up the bottle, unscrewed the cap, and took a long sip. "How long have you been living here?"

"Since last … September. After I moved out of Dash's place."

She wrinkled her nose. "So almost ten months."

He shrugged. "I guess so. Why?"

"No furniture anywhere but this room and the kitchen table and chairs?" She raised her eyebrows.

He shook his head. "I told you, I'm not sure where I want to end up. The city, here… I'm renting and I'm over at Dash's and Xander's a lot. I don't entertain. I didn't *need* anything else." He reached out and put his hand on her arm. "What's going on in that head of yours?"

"Nothing … everything." She turned to face him better, dislodging his touch. "You say you want us to try again. You're talking about making love, which sounds like you want a future. But you're not settled in your life. You're still a man on tour with no home base, no sense of home, and I want that in a partner. I *need* that. I need someone responsible."

He blinked. "Responsible. Like you were last night? Drunk at a bar, lucky your brother-in-law was there or that you happened to drunk text me?"

Her cheeks pinkened in embarrassment, which was the last thing he wanted her to feel. "Tara, listen to me. The past ten months, I've been working nonstop in the studio with the guys. I needed to cement my place in the band. To become an integral part of them. That's where my focus has been. Not on decorating a house I'm barely in."

She wrapped her arms around herself. "And it doesn't matter anyway because your next step is to go on tour, right? So maybe *responsible* was the wrong word, but *stable* is not." She drew a deep breath and let it out again. "Ever since I lost my dad … suddenly … my life has been one major change after another."

"Tara–"

She shook her head. "Let me finish, please?"

He nodded. "Go on."

"I thought I'd go to school in New York, come home to California, and take over Dad's practice. There were other vets there to keep the business running until I got my degree, but Mom wanted to start over somewhere new. So New York became home, she remarried, and I had stepsiblings. I've just begun to settle in."

She paused in thought, and he waited her out this time, knowing she wasn't finished and needed to explain.

She rubbed her eyes with her palms before pulling herself together again, straightening her shoulders and meeting his gaze. "Look, I told myself if I got involved with anyone, it would be someone who wants the same things I do."

He grasped one of her hands and held on so she couldn't pull away. "And what is that?"

"A house and a family of my own. Someone I can count on, who will be there."

Because she'd lost her father, she equated stability with the idea of a traditional family, he thought. But it didn't have to be that way.

"Look at Dash and Cassidy. They're going to make it work when he goes on tour. Plenty of famous musicians have families and a home base. Just because I don't have one yet doesn't mean I don't want the same things you do." And he only wanted them with her.

Was it fast? Yeah. Was it crazy? Probably. Did he care? Fuck no.

Though she was listening, he knew she wasn't processing his words. "We don't need to move so quickly. Let's keep getting to know each other, okay?" He tugged on her hand. "Let me take you out again. No pressure for anything more."

Obviously between their deep connection in bed and his ridiculous empty rental, she'd gotten scared and was pulling back. He couldn't change his career, nor did he want to. He also didn't believe she'd ask that of him. He needed to be part of her life so he could show her they could have the future she wanted. Even if his touring meant their way of going about it was untraditional.

"So what do you say?" he asked in the wake of her silence. "We can go on another date sometime this week?"

"Yeah, okay." She bit down on her lower lip. "But I think I should go now."

He took the win where he could. "Okay." Leaning over, he pressed a kiss to her lips and then stood up to get dressed and take her home.

Chapter Seven

After Axel drove Tara home, he returned to his house, more aware of the empty living, dining, and family rooms. As he walked toward his bedroom, Tara's words echoed in his head.

You're not settled in your life. You're still a man on tour with no home base, no sense of home, and I want that in a partner. I need that. I need someone responsible.

He was forced to admit the truth stung, and he couldn't sort through his thoughts on his own. He needed to talk to someone who knew him well, and nobody understood him better than Cassidy. He showered, ate breakfast, and called his sister. Despite it being a Sunday, she was at Sasha and Xander's going over work, and he headed there for a visit.

Sasha let him in and greeted him with a welcoming hug. The famous actress never ceased to amaze him in how much she looked like the girl next door when not in full makeup. She was exceptionally pretty in her California blond way, and he knew how much Xander loved her.

She led him into the kitchen, where the women had been working, his buddy Bella included.

He kissed his sister on the cheek and gave the dog a pat on the head. "Miss me, girl?"

"We just saw you last night," Cassidy said, laughing. "But if your best friend didn't miss you, don't worry. I did."

He rolled his eyes. "Fine. Make fun of me. I'm used to it."

Sasha grinned at their byplay. "Listen, I can give you two some privacy," she offered, rising from her seat.

He thought about it and shook his head. Both Cassidy and Sasha knew what it took to build a stable relationship. He might as well get advice from them both. "I appreciate it. Especially since it's your house, but stay, please. I could use your opinion, too."

"Okay then, sit and let's talk," Sasha said with a smile.

Cassidy rested her arms on the table and met his gaze. "Talk to me."

It was so unlike him to discuss his personal life with a woman mostly because he'd never had one before. Unless you counted the groupies, which he didn't.

"Let me make it easier for you. It's about Tara, right?" Sasha asked.

He released the breath he'd been holding and nodded. "She doesn't think I can give her what she needs. She wants stability and someone she can count on. When she looks at me, all she sees is a guy who rents a house he's barely in, lives with no furniture, and goes on tour in between writing albums. And I didn't see it before, but when she laid it out like that … she had a point." He reached down and scratched Bella's head, and she stepped closer, placing her chin on his thigh.

Cassidy and Sasha glanced at each other, but his sister spoke first. "What do *you* want?"

"Tara. And I'm willing to do whatever it takes except give up my career." Bella nuzzled her nose into his side, and he slid his hand over her fur.

"You should get a dog," Sasha said. And before he could reply, she held up a hand. "Hear me out. You adore Bella. I mean, you're certainly not here all the time to pet Xander." She snickered at her joke. "But seriously, what shows permanence and commitment as much as getting a dog?"

He raised his eyebrows. He couldn't deny how much he'd love his own pet and had even thought about it. He also knew all the reasons it wasn't a good idea. "I travel and I'm not around when I tour."

"I'm around and I'm happy to take care of your dog," his sister said.

"And I have to take care of Bella anyway. If I have to be on a movie set, I have a kennel I trust for short visits," Sasha added.

Axel shook his head. "You two are crazy."

"But smart. You want to show Tara you can offer stability, a dog is a start," Cassidy said.

"And Tara is a vet. What other way to her heart than a dog?" Sasha shrugged. "Seems like common sense to me."

"Are you two always this good at tag teaming?"

"They're masters." Xander strode into the kitchen. His glasses were on, indicating he'd been writing, and he headed to the fridge, pulling out a can of soda. "Anyone want some?"

"No, thanks," Axel said.

The women shook their heads.

"So what's going on in here?" He walked over to the table, pulled out a chair beside Sasha, and sat, straddling it. "What are you two up to?"

"Convincing your brother to get a dog," Sasha said.

"So he'll stop coming by all the time?" Xander grinned as he spoke.

"No, so he can impress Tara," Cassidy said, making Axel feel like the asshole under the microscope.

And when Xander burst out laughing, Axel glared at them all. But at least he had a plan forming, not just for his next date with Tara but beyond.

* * * *

Tara had a jam-packed day of appointments that ended with an emergency for a patient that had gotten into chocolate, which was toxic to dogs. The poor pup needed to be given medicine that would cause him to vomit, hooked up to an IV, pumped full of fluids, and treated with activated charcoal to prevent the chocolate from entering his bloodstream. Lucky, the dog, needed to stay overnight, and Tara and Harry had a technician who would check in on the inpatients during the night.

Though she hadn't finished up late, she was exhausted and didn't remember she had a date with Axel until almost six. Not that she'd forgotten about him completely. He'd been on her mind since he'd rescued her this past Saturday night. An evening she didn't want to repeat. She was too old to wake up hung over. But not too old to find herself underneath Axel.

As she took her cosmetic case into the bathroom and touched up her makeup, her thoughts drifted to Axel and the way he'd felt deep inside her. She recalled him pushing into her, his erection pulsing, her body responding, and desire rippled through her and her panties grew damp. She shifted her legs but couldn't alleviate the need those memories inspired.

And when she allowed them to wash over her, the emotions flowed, as well. Axel had pulled up the feelings she'd locked down after he'd left for Los Angeles and her father died. From the way he held her and looked into her eyes, everything he did told her she was special to him. How could she not *feel* again?

She placed the mascara wand down on the counter and looked in the mirror, seeing the girl who'd fallen in love with Axel and not the woman who'd sworn never to let in anyone who could hurt her again. And that was dangerous to her heart.

Especially since she'd seen the evidence of his transitory nature. Who lived for so long without a sofa? A television? Pictures on the walls? Though she hadn't mentioned it, she'd taken a look around his room, and there was just one photo on his dresser. Him with his grandmother and sister. No other personal items with sentimental value to be found.

Back when they were in high school, his grandmother had kept his music awards and any accolades hanging in his room. After she'd died, he hadn't taken them down. His way of keeping her memory alive. But it seemed like, over the years, personal items no longer meant anything to him. *Furniture* didn't mean anything to him, almost as if he had one foot out the door already.

It didn't make sense. Nothing about the house he rented or the life he lived jibed with the man who was trying to convince her to give *them* another chance.

Maybe that was why she was going out with him again. Not to mention, she couldn't deny the pull he had over her, how much she enjoyed his company, and the sexual chemistry she'd never felt for anyone else. But she couldn't let him hurt her again.

Pushing the confusing thoughts out of her head, she picked up the wand and put two coats of mascara on her lashes, swiped some blush on her cheeks, and added her favorite shimmery gloss to her lips.

She'd caught a ride with her mom this morning so Axel could pick her up for their date from work. A last glance in the mirror and she was ready.

She walked into the outer office to find her mom putting on a light sweater as she prepared to leave. "Finished for the day?" Tara asked.

Her mom turned to face her. "Glenn and I have dinner plans," she said. "You look pretty. I take it you have plans of your own?"

"Thank you and yes, I do."

"With Axel?" her mother asked, the hope in her voice evident.

Tara nodded. "But don't go getting your hopes up, okay?" The last thing she needed was her mother being disappointed when things didn't work out after Axel went back on tour.

"Amy told me he drove you home after the party." Her mother's way of digging for information.

She couldn't help but smile. "He did, and I appreciated him rescuing me from myself."

Her mother eyed her, doing her obvious best to figure out what Tara was thinking. "I'm just glad you're going out," she said at last.

Tara let out a long breath, glad they weren't going to be having a deep talk about feelings and Tara's dating life. Or worse, discussing her sex life.

"Thanks, Mom." She glanced out the window and saw Axel pull into the parking lot.

Wanting to avoid her mother's interrogation, she walked over and kissed her mom on the cheek. "Say hi to Glenn for me. I see Axel's car. I'll see you tomorrow."

Before her mother could reply, Tara waved and rushed for the door.

She stepped outside at the same time Axel climbed out of his convertible. "No need to get out. I'm here and ready."

"I can still open your door for you." He grinned, looking sexy as ever in his jeans, a navy tee, and sunglasses tucked into the round collar of his shirt.

He stopped her before she could pass him and head to the passenger side, placing his hands on her waist. "Hello, Tara." He dipped his head and kissed her lips.

A little happy sigh escaped. Dammit. "Hi, yourself," she said as he lifted his mouth from hers.

With his hand on her back, he walked her around the back end of the car, opened the door, and helped her in, shutting the door.

He climbed into the driver seat and turned on the engine.

"Where are we going?" she asked.

He placed an arm on her seat, turning her way. "Depends on you. Are you hungry?"

Her grumbling stomach answered for her. "Starving. I barely had time for lunch."

"How's pizza?"

"That sounds perfect."

He nodded, and a few minutes later, they pulled into the parking lot of her favorite pizza place. They ordered quickly, and since the place wasn't packed, the food came out fast.

She glanced at him, taking a sip of her soda. "I'm going to apologize ahead of time," she said, picking up a slice, taking a bite, and moaning at the cheesy flavor. She chewed, swallowed, and repeated, until she'd nearly finished the one slice in record time.

She wasn't even embarrassed.

It wasn't until she finished, drank some more, and looked up that she noticed him watching her, a huge smile on his handsome face.

"You weren't kidding about being starving. I think you need to make time for food. It's not good for you to be that hungry."

She nodded. "I know, but sometimes there are emergencies, and the day just gets away from me. Did you guys work in the studio today?" she asked as she took another slice.

This time he picked up a piece for himself. "We've been working on music since I joined the band." He took a bite, taking the time to chew and swallow. "The guys had songs ready, and I had to learn those and give my two cents because … that's me. Then we wrote together, used some, tossed more… Today we finished the final song for the album." He followed that up with another bite.

"He says so easily." She studied him, proud of all he'd accomplished. "You're amazing, Axel. You've really achieved your dreams."

"Not all of them," he said, meeting her gaze and holding hers captive so she was unable to look away.

His expression was serious, his lips in a set line, obviously attempting to impart a serious tone to their night.

She didn't want that kind of date. "What are we doing after pizza?" she asked, breaking the spell he'd woven over her.

He blinked and refocused, shaking his head before he replied. "It's a surprise but I promise it's right up your alley."

She wondered what he had in mind.

"If you want to find out, finish eating so we can get going," he said, his easy grin back on his face.

A little while later, she was beyond full, the kind of full where she'd eaten faster than she'd digested and now regretted the last slice. He paid, signed autographs for a group of teenage girls who'd walked in, and they headed outside.

"Come on. Let's walk," he said, clasping her hand in his.

They strode along the sidewalk, talking about her day and Lucky, the dog who'd eaten chocolate, until Axel stopped in front of the pet store at the end of the row of stores where the pizza place was located.

"We're here." He looked through the window that had puppies playing in shredded paper, bouncing around each other.

"Why?" Confused, she turned to stare him and not the adorable dogs who were no doubt from a puppy mill and whose poor mother would still be there, suffering.

"I want to get a dog."

She blinked. There was so much wrong with that statement she didn't know where to begin. "I don't… A dog? You're never home."

He frowned. "Give me some credit for thinking things through. I can bring the dog to Dash's when we're working so he or she isn't alone. I spoke to Brent, our assistant, and he's more than happy to watch out for him when we're locked in the studio."

She nodded, acknowledging he'd thought *some things* through. "And when you're on tour?"

He winced at that question. "Cassidy and Sasha said they could take over. Or I could hire a pet sitter or live-in house sitter to help out, too." He shrugged. "I love animals, Tara. You know that from when were together last. Ask Xander how much time I spend at his place just so I can hang out with Bella."

"I'm not denying you'd be a great doggie daddy but … does your lease allow for pets?" In the house with no furniture?

He nodded. "Yeah, it does. But like I told you, that's not my permanent place. I'll be buying something soon."

She bit down on her cheek. "Okay. You're serious about this, then?"

"As a heart attack."

She shook her head and looked at the cute puppies once more. "Then brace yourself for a lecture," she said and explained to him about her *adopt, don't shop* philosophy and why. "So in my opinion, you should go to a shelter. Unless you have allergies and need a purebred dog that doesn't shed and is as close to hypoallergenic as you can get, in which case, I recommend a breeder."

By the time she finished her long spiel, he was smiling and nodding in agreement. "So take me to the shelter."

"Now?"

He nodded. "I told you, I want a dog." His expression was earnest, his tone serious. He looked like an adorable kid who couldn't wait to get his pet.

"Okay, look. I volunteer at Norah's Ark Rescue. I can call and see if Norah stayed late so we can stop by." She pulled out her phone and made the call.

Next thing she knew, she and Axel were standing in the parking lot. She'd spent the ride over trying to understand his sudden need for a dog.

"Axel, wait." She placed a hand on his arm. "Why are you doing this?" The only reason she'd come up with was that he was trying to make a good impression on her. Why else would a man who lived the way he did suddenly want a pet?

He tipped his head to one side. "After you left, I looked around the house and saw it for the first time. I realized you're right. It's ridiculous I haven't put down roots in any way. And I've been lonely, but I haven't bothered to look into why. I just kept going to Xander's… I mean, Dash set that example, but I bonded with Bella. So I decided I need a dog of my own." He shrugged as if the simple answer made sense.

She supposed it did. "I'm just worried you don't realize the work that goes along with owning a dog, and I'd hate for you to pass all the responsibility off to someone you pay to take care of the pet for you."

He shoved his hands into his jeans pockets. "I've been with you long enough in the past to know what responsibility means. Despite what you said on Sunday or think today."

At that moment, she realized she'd hurt his feelings, and that had been the last thing she wanted to do. Stepping forward, she cupped his face in her hand. "I'm sorry. I never meant to insult you. Not over the weekend and not now." She sighed. "In my profession, I see too many people take on the responsibility, then dump an animal when they realize all the work and money pet ownership entails."

He smiled, and it wasn't the smart-aleck grin or the sexy lift of his lips. It was a genuine expression of feeling. "That might be the nicest thing you've said to me since we saw each other again."

He leaned in and captured her lips with his, immediately deepening the kiss. She lost herself in the sweep of his tongue and the meshing of their mouths, forgetting everything except Axel and the way he made her feel.

He slid his hands around her waist, his palms cupping her ass as he pulled her against him. The hardness of his erection pressed into her belly, and she groaned just as a car honked in the distance.

Reminded they weren't in a private place, she broke the kiss and touched her forehead to his chest. "You make me forget where I am," she said. He even caused her to overlook who she was and what she wanted.

"It's not a bad thing to get lost in each other." He stepped back, placed his hand under her chin, and forced her to meet his gaze. "I'm not going to hurt you." Those dazzling green orbs captured her, his deep tone begging her to trust him.

"Let's go get you a dog," she murmured, grasping his hand and leading him inside. The bells over the door rang as they entered.

She'd spent enough time in the rescue building that the citrus scent of enzymatic cleaner was familiar to her. She approached the empty desk, knowing Norah must be in the back and she'd come out soon.

She glanced at Axel, hoping he knew what he was getting himself into with a pet.

"My favorite doctor is here!" Norah rushed out of the back room.

Tara had taken to her, with her pink hair and bubbly personality, the day they'd met. And vice versa.

"Hi!" Tara walked around the counter and hugged the woman she considered more than a colleague. "Norah, this is my … friend–"

"Her boyfriend," Axel said.

Ignoring him and the flutter in her stomach his words caused, she continued, "This is Axel Forrester. Axel, this is Norah. She owns the shelter."

A trust fund baby with a heart of gold, Norah had taken the money left to her by her grandparents and opened the rescue.

Norah looked Axel over, no doubt because of their contradicting descriptions of their relationship.

"You're the drummer from Caged Chaos and now the Original Kings," she said, her tone and grin those of an excited fan.

"Watch it. His ego is big enough," Tara said, laughing.

Axel walked over and shook her hand. "Nice to meet you."

"Same here." Norah smiled.

"Tara was just educating me on the *adopt, don't shop* philosophy, and I have to admit, now that I understand, it makes perfect sense," he said.

Tara shot him a surprised glance. Even when he'd agreed to come to the shelter instead of the pet store, she really thought he'd been trying to make a good impression on her. Instead, he'd not only listened, he'd taken her words to heart. And her own heart squeezed in her chest.

If she wasn't careful, he'd win her over despite all the reasons she was trying hard not to fall.

Chapter Eight

Norah pulled out paperwork and placed it on the counter. "Sorry. We're not technology based. You'll need to fill these out before you leave with a dog. Usually there's a screening process, but I think we can trust the word of our resident vet." She grinned at Tara.

"I'll do that," he said, picking up the pen and answering the questions as the women spoke.

"How's the fundraising going?" Tara asked, causing his ears to perk up.

Norah let out a sigh. "Unfortunately, not as well as I'd like. I don't want to have to close this place in the off months, but I don't know if I can afford to keep it going if nobody pitches in." Norah shrugged. "I put in as much money as I could on my own, but things are tight."

"You're having financial problems?" he asked as he scrawled his name on the final page.

Norah glanced up. "Yes. I started the shelter with my inheritance, but it's expensive to keep the place up and running without substantial donations." She pulled out a set of keys. "Ready to check out the dogs?"

Obviously she didn't want to discuss her business problems, and he respected that. They followed Norah to the door leading to the back kennels.

She paused before letting them in. "So what kind of dog are you looking for? Big, small, medium? Hair, fur?"

He looked to Tara, aware he must have a confused expression on his face. He hadn't thought about the kind of dog he wanted.

She laughed and patted his shoulder. "He loves a friend's golden retriever, so he's comfortable with that size and type of fur. Beyond that, let's see who he takes to and who takes to him."

No sooner had Norah opened the door than a cacophony of barking sounded loudly around them, all the dogs making their excited presence known.

As they walked past the runs, rooms, and cages, a knot formed in his stomach at the number of unwanted dogs. "I wish I could take them all," he said over the noise.

Tara put her hand on his shoulder. "I know how you feel. Every time I come in to do a check on a new or sick animal, I want to bring them all home. But for now, Dakota is enough."

"I still need to meet her," he said, determined to be part of everything in her life.

"We'll do that. Now look around and see who draws you." She spoke into his ear, and his body reacted to her nearness and warm breath.

Reaching over, he slid his hand into hers. "Let's walk."

They passed large breeds, small and medium breeds, exuberant dogs, and dogs who hung back, watching warily. He strode up and down the aisle, taking in one side of the cages and then the other.

He paused by a solitary black and white dog with silky fur and big puppy eyes. With a black head and a white stripe along the nose and a white body, the dog was … special. Their gazes met and held.

"That's a pointer/border collie mix," Norah said, coming up behind them. "He's a large breed. Currently weighs fifty-five pounds, and his name is Walter."

As she explained, Axel and Walter experienced some kind of serious bonding moment. This dog spoke to him without words.

"He's an owner surrender," Norah went on. "The family had to move away and into a small apartment. Walter has a lot of energy, and they couldn't meet his needs."

Axel stared at the dog. "Can you open the gate?"

As Norah let him into the run, she said, "I should warn you, he's a" — the dog immediately began to rub up against his jeans — "clinger," she said, laughing.

Axel knelt down, and Walter leaned farther into him, rubbing his head into Axel's stomach. In that instant, Axel knew in his heart this was his dog. The only problem was, much like his previous owners, Axel wouldn't be around to give the dog the attention and exercise he'd undoubtedly need for his energy level. Though he seemed mellow now, Axel had no doubt Norah knew what she was talking about.

Though he intended to buy a big house, what would happen when he was away on tour, like Tara had asked? When she'd laid it out for him in the parking lot, he hadn't wanted to admit she had a point. But faced with the dog he wanted with every fiber of his being, Axel couldn't be selfish.

He rose slowly and turned to Tara.

"What's wrong?" she asked before he could speak. "Is he not the right dog?" Concern wrinkled the corners of her eyes.

He glanced down at Walter, who was still rubbing against him like a cat, claiming him in every way. "No, he's perfect." And Axel had a goddamned lump in his throat.

He swallowed hard. "I can't take him. You were right. I'm not in any position to bring a dog home. I was listening to Norah talk about his previous family and all they couldn't give him, and it made me realize I'm no better. I might have the space for him, but it's not fair to bring him home and pawn him off on Cassidy or Sasha. He's had enough upheaval in his short life."

Tara glanced at Norah, then hooked her arm into Axel's and led him out of the dog pen, down the hall, and out into the main room. "I'm sorry," she murmured.

He shook his head. "You tried to tell me." It hurt like hell to walk away from Walter. Axel wanted to pull the dog into his arms and give him the home he deserved.

"Let's get out of here." He glanced at Norah. "Sorry to have wasted your time."

She treated him to an understanding smile. "I'd prefer you realize now rather than later and have him go through yet another home before being returned here."

"Thanks, Norah. I'll see you on my regular day." Tara waved, and they walked out into the muggy air.

They stopped by the car, and she tapped his arm. "I'm sorry," she said again.

He didn't have any words for what he was feeling.

"Do you want to come back to my place and meet Dakota? Or is it the wrong time?" she asked.

He might be in a shit mood, but he wouldn't turn down spending time with Tara or meeting her dog. His *get a pet plan* might have imploded, but his *win over Tara* agenda hadn't changed.

****

Tara sensed Axel's mood and remained quiet on the drive to her house. Despite knowing he'd done the right thing, her heart hurt because he'd so obviously bonded with Walter. Axel parked in her driveway, and she slipped her hand into his as they walked to her front door.

"Hang on." She opened her purse and sorted through her stuff, finding her key.

No sooner had she opened the door than Dakota came barreling toward them, a white ball of fur jumping on Axel with her front paws.

"Dakota, off," Tara said as she shut the door behind them.

The well-trained dog immediately placed all four paws on the floor. Tara hadn't been able to train the greeting out of her, but she listened once she'd said hello.

She kicked off her shoes by the door, then glanced at Dash, wondering if he'd care that he now had white fur on his black clothes. But he was already kneeling on the floor, giving her baby a huge greeting that would only make the hair situation worse. Question answered, she mused.

Though Dakota greeted everyone warmly, she was good at getting a sense of people and turning her back if she didn't like how she was treated. No worries here. If her paws on his shoulders were anything to go by, she and Axel were now best buds.

Amused, Tara leaned against the wall, watching them for a minute before she was ready to move things along. "Let's relax in another room or she's going to think you're her new playmate."

Axel's gaze met hers and laughter danced in his eyes. "Jealous that another girl is paying attention to me?"

She rolled her eyes. "Are you seriously asking me if I'm jealous of my dog?"

He rose to his feet and walked toward her. She took one step back and came up against the wall, aware of his large body so close to hers.

"I'm sorry about Walter," she said softly.

He nodded. "I should have listened to you. You know what you're talking about, and you know what? Maybe a part of me did want the dog to get your approval, at least at first."

It impressed her that he admitted the truth. "Until you met him," she murmured, lifting her hand and cupping his cheek. "Pets have a way of burrowing into our hearts."

He touched his forehead to hers. "Not just pets."

They remained like that, their breaths mingling, so many words between them unsaid.

Maybe they needed to be spoken out loud. "It feels like this is moving so fast I can't keep up," she said.

"Because when we're together it's like no time has passed." He placed his hand beneath her chin and tilted her head up so she met his gaze. "Stop overthinking, Tara. Let those walls down," he said in a husky voice.

Oh, God. She really couldn't resist him. Rising onto her tiptoes, she pressed her lips to his, and he let out a low groan. Next thing she knew, he lifted her, and she wrapped her legs around his waist, holding on. She buried her face in the crook of his neck and breathed in his scent, one she dreamed about every night when she was alone.

"Bedroom?" he asked.

She directed him, and he carried her to her room with determined strides. "Close the door or we'll have company you don't want."

He kicked the door shut behind them. "Unless you're replacing me as your girlfriend with Dakota?" She laughed at the thought but sobered quickly as her chest rubbed against his, her nipples feeling the pressure of his hard body as she moved.

"You're irreplaceable," he said, tossing her onto the bed.

She bounced and glanced up to find his expression filled with yearning.

He clasped her legs and yanked her closer to the edge of the mattress, making her wonder what he had planned. Nothing prepared her for the moment he grasped the sides of her button-down shirt and yanked, sending the buttons flying.

She gasped in surprise but had to admit she found his determination hot, and her core pulsed with need. He pulled one cup of her bra down and latched on to her nipple with his mouth, sucking until her sex practically vibrated with each tug of his lips and scrape of his teeth.

Writhing on the mattress, she tried to hold on to the covers but couldn't get a grip, so she pulled on his hair instead. She couldn't decide if she was urging him on or trying to escape the intensity of feelings he aroused. As if he knew she couldn't take any more, he switched to the other breast, giving it the same treatment until she thought she might come from his mouth on her nipples alone.

"I need you inside me." Her body wouldn't let her deny what it wanted.

"I like you bossy." He stood upright, pulling her to a sitting position. "Now strip."

She raised an eyebrow. "Now who's bossy?" she asked as he watched, waiting for her to move.

She shrugged off her blouse, unhooked and slid off her bra. Only then did he shed his T-shirt, unbutton, unzip, and tug down his jeans and boxer briefs. His shoes were already kicked to the side, and his clothes quickly joined them.

Trying not to get sidetracked by his thick, erect cock, which she desperately wanted to feel inside her, she worked on her slacks and managed to slide them, along with her underwear, down to her ankles. He grabbed hold and pulled, adding them to his garments on the floor.

Then he stood between her legs, his erection gripped in his hand, when it dawned on her.

"We need a condom," she said.

He winced. "Shit. I didn't bring one." He studied her intently and then spoke. "I haven't been with anyone in over six months, and I've had a physical since then. I'm clean."

She swallowed hard. When they were together last, they'd always used protection. They'd been young, not stupid. And she'd never slept with a man unless he wore a condom.

"I'm on the pill," she whispered.

"So I guess the question is, do you trust me?" As he asked, he lazily pumped his cock in his hand, his jaw tight as he worked his grip up and down.

His lean, strong, muscled body exuded want and sex appeal, but beyond the physical, what he was asking her went deeper. If she said yes, if she felt him bare, it would change her. It would change *them*.

"I trust that you're telling me the truth." She swiped her tongue over her lips. "I'm struggling with what saying yes would mean." He deserved nothing but honesty.

His eyes glittered as he met her gaze. "It would mean *everything*. I want you to trust me not just with your body but with your heart."

Well, that was putting it out there, she thought, her pulse picking up speed.

"I want you to believe I'll never intentionally hurt you. I won't cheat when I'm on the road. I don't know how long the touring part of the Original Kings will last, but it won't be every year. I'll talk to Dash and see if he's ready to cut back some. I'll give you everything you want for your future because I want the same things, but only with you."

Her mouth parted, and she stared up at the man she'd once dreamed would be her future, even as she knew they could never make it work. She'd been fighting him from the day he walked back into her life, and she understood why. She'd lost Axel, then not long after, her father's death had left her with abandonment issues that ran deep.

Now she had to choose. Let him in, in every way, or continue to protect herself and never know true happiness. She'd watched her mother conquer her grief and move on. Was she going to doom herself to a life of loneliness?

He held out a hand, silently asking for … everything.

She drew a deep breath and took that final leap, linking her hand in his.

"Thank fuck," he said, the relief in his tone palpable. The husky desire in his voice renewed her own.

She wasn't sure who moved first, but he fell on top of her, his lips consuming hers, their kiss more open, honest, and giving than anything she'd felt before.

He helped her slide back to the center of the bed and rose over her, his cock once again in his hand, this time at her pulsing, needy core.

"You're mine. You've always been mine," he said and slid into her, filling her, consuming her.

He was smooth and hot inside her, and with nothing between them, they bonded in ways that surpassed sex and broke through the concrete wall she'd built around her heart.

Chapter Nine

Axel woke up wrapped around Tara. For the first time in forever, all was right in his world. Since he didn't want to wake her, he had a long time to think about everything that had happened yesterday and how quickly things had done a one-eighty. Walter was still in the kennel, which broke his damned heart, but the woman he loved was in his arms.

Given the choice, things had worked out in his favor, but he wished he could help those dogs find homes and Norah save the shelter. Ideas came and went as Tara slept, some sticking and helping him form a game plan.

Once he'd worked out those issues, his thoughts turned to Tara. He breathed her in, inhaling the strawberry scent of her shampoo and the lingering hint of sex in the air. Last night had been a reunion of the best kind. After that first time, they'd fallen asleep. He'd woken her at three with his face in her pussy and his name on her lips, and after an explosive orgasm where he thought she'd pulled out all of his hair, she'd greedily returned the favor. He'd come harder than he ever had in his life, and he grinned at the memory.

He didn't know how he'd convinced her to trust him, and as she stirred, he was worried she'd wake up and regret that she'd given herself to him in the deepest way. He'd made himself clear he wanted everything, and he hadn't been kidding.

She rolled until she was facing him, and her lashes fluttered open, her brown-eyed stare as enticing as his morning coffee.

"Hey," she said, one side of her face on the pillow as she met his gaze.

"Hey." He brushed long strands of hair off her cheek. "Sleep well?"

A pleased, sated smile took hold. "Really well."

"No regrets?" He had to ask.

She placed her finger over his lips, stopping the question. "Not one."

He blew out a relieved breath. "I need to know what changed your mind."

She sighed and placed her hand over his chest. "You asked me to trust you with my heart. You wanted everything, and I knew if I walked away, I was going to be alone. Worse, I'd be without you again."

He saw the sheen of tears in her eyes before she blinked them away. He never wanted to see her sad or hurting.

"I knew my mother had loved and lost my dad, and she'd moved on. There was a lesson there I was finally willing to see." Her fingers drew circles on his skin. "So I opened my eyes. I needed to get over my fear of loss and abandonment or I'd lose you. And I couldn't let you go again."

He'd heard what he needed to. There was no going back. For either of them. He kissed her hard, his mouth parting her lips, his tongue making itself at home.

He wasn't sure how long they lay locked and lost in each other, but when she broke the kiss and came up for air, he looked her in the eyes. "I love you, Tara. I'll be with you even when I'm not, and I'll never be gone long."

Her smile lit up everything inside him. "I've made my peace with what I thought were our differences. I fell in love with a boy who wanted to be a famous rock musician, and I'm still in love with the man who achieved his dream."

He grasped her wrist. "I'm going to make all of your dreams come true, too."

"You already have."

* * * *

A week later, the sun shone overhead, a gift from above on the day of an outdoor concert. The band tested their instruments, which had been tuned and left ready for them on stage.

Axel had made miracles happen. He'd arranged for the Original Kings to play a benefit concert to raise money for Norah's Ark in order to keep the shelter open and get some of the pets adopted.

While he had his plan, Tara had hers. She'd gone behind his back and taken care of something very important before it was too late, and she had the surprise waiting for him when he came off stage. From the moment of his return, he'd been all about giving to her. It was time she did something for him.

Norah joined her at the moment the band struck their opening chord. Around her, the Kingston family mingled with each other, excited to see Dash in his element. Just like Tara couldn't wait to see Axel in his.

Watching him play, sweat gleaming on his strong muscles, his talent on the drums bordering legendary, she couldn't be prouder. She would have been a fool to push him away and was so grateful she'd come to her senses. When it came to loss, the past was difficult to overcome, but this man and the life they could have together were worth it.

Later, after the band played their final encore and Dash encouraged the crowd to donate to the shelter and to *adopt, not shop*, the guys laid down their instruments and walked off stage to a standing ovation. Well, the audience was already standing anyway, she thought, smiling.

"Tara?"

She turned at the sound of her name. A woman who resembled the Kingston siblings and had to be their mother walked over to her. "Hi. I'm Melly Kingston."

"Hello! I've heard so much about you." Tara smiled at the other woman. "Axel has told me how you've treated him like family since he joined the band and his sister married Dash. It's so good to meet you in person."

Melly met her gaze. "Can we hug? I feel like you're family now, too."

Tara hugged the woman who had treated Axel like a son.

"I'm glad you two are together now," Melly said. "It wasn't that long ago he was climbing the walls, wondering how to convince you he was serious about you." Melly's warmth made her impossible not to like.

"Well, we had our challenges," Tara admitted. "Mostly mine."

"But she came to her senses, and now they can live happily ever after," a familiar voice said as her mom wrapped an arm around Tara's shoulders.

Tara turned and kissed her mother's cheek. "Mom, this is Melly Kingston." Tara performed the introductions, and the women started talking. "If you two don't mind, I have something important I need to do." Tara left them alone, sensing the two would get along well.

She headed toward the stage at the same time Axel, still in his sweaty T-shirt, came bounding toward her, obviously still amped up from the performance. "I'd say we rocked the house," he said with a pleased grin.

"Yes, Mr. Ego, you did."

He swept her into his arms and sealed his lips over hers. He kissed her long, hard, and deep, and totally too much for a public place, but she got lost in him anyway.

By the time he let her up, she was breathless. "I love what you did for the shelter. I can't thank you enough."

"No need to thank me. It's a worthy cause." He hooked an arm around her waist. "Besides, I'd do anything for you."

"And I'd do anything for you. Which brings me to my surprise for you."

He narrowed his gaze. "You can't have a surprise for me. I have one for you."

She shook her head. "Nope. You aren't going to one-up me, Axel Forrester."

He lifted his shirt and wiped the sweat from his face with the material.

Her gaze fell to his six-pack, and she was surprised she wasn't drooling. "Stop trying to distract me," she said.

He laughed and whispered, "We could leave now. Nobody would know."

She shook her head. "Not yet. Surprise, remember? Come on." As she led him to the parking lot, she began to explain. "Since we are together…" They were alternating staying in the gatehouse on her family's property and in his empty house that he still refused to decorate.

Neither of which was ideal, but that was a discussion for another time. "I figured that I would add to your stability factor."

They reached the lot where Norah and her volunteers had the puppies who were available for adoption. Nobody could just take a dog home today, but they could meet the dogs, fill out an application, and be vetted afterwards. Then someone would call them if they were approved as a pet owner.

"Stability factor?" He came to a halt. "I thought we were past those issues." Panic seemed to invade his expression.

"*We* are. Relax." She put a hand on his chest to reassure him. "This is a good surprise. I just meant that we're living together, and I'm around to take care of a pet when you're on tour. No upheaval involved."

"I don't understand."

"You will." She led him around the booth and paused where a large crate sat alone with a black and white dog inside who appeared disinterested in everything going on around him.

"Walter?" Axel asked, excitement in his tone.

The dog's ears perked up at the sound of his name.

Smiling, she watched as Axel walked over and the dog's long tail began to wag as he pawed at the kennel gate to get to Axel.

"Is he up for adoption here?" Axel asked.

"He's taken," she said, carefully watching Axel's face. He didn't seem to understand yet, and she couldn't torture him another second. "Baby, open the crate and take out your dog."

His gaze swung to hers. "You…?"

She nodded.

"What about Dakota? Will they get along?" he asked, his body vibrating with contained happiness.

"Well, I've had them play together a couple of times this week, and I even brought Walter home to make sure there were no immediate territorial issues." When Axel had been in the studio with the band, rehearsing. "They got along great. So go get your dog!"

Axel's gaze swung from Walter, who was still pawing at the crate, to her, as if unsure of who he should hug first.

"Go!" She waved a hand toward Walter.

Axel let his new dog out of the crate and dropped to his knees,

Walter immediately nuzzling his head into Axel's stomach.

Tara stepped behind the makeshift tables and booth and pulled out a leash from a box. Walking over to her man and their dog, she clipped the leash onto Walter's collar, one she'd already gotten for him.

"My mission here is complete," she said, handing him the leash.

Axel rose to his feet. "But mine isn't. I told you I have a surprise, too, remember?" He reached into his pocket and pulled out a key.

She wrinkled her nose in confusion.

"In case you think I don't listen, you need to know that I do. You wanted stability. A house. Kids. A future. I don't know about you, but I want to have you to myself for a bit before we have kids. I plan to marry you, so don't worry about that. But I refuse to live in your mother and stepdad's gatehouse, and my rental isn't right for us. So I took it upon myself to change our living situation."

She narrowed her gaze. "You did … what?"

"I bought a house that you're going to decorate. Or get help decorating. Whatever. In other words, I also took care of our stability situation." He grinned, obviously pleased with himself.

She flung her arms around his neck and kissed his cheek over and over.

"You don't care that you didn't see it first?" he asked warily.

"I trust you, remember? It's not my parents' house, it's not your empty house…"

"It's on the beach on the other side of Xander's." His grin widened, and she couldn't help but chuckle.

Xander's reaction would be something different, she was sure. "How did you manage this in under a week?" she asked.

Laughing, he said, "Let's just say I made the owner an offer he couldn't refuse. And they were so happy, they agreed to move out by this weekend."

Her eyes opened wide. "That must have been some offer."

He waved a hand through the air. "It's just money. I have it, and I can spend it. And now we have everything we ever wanted," he said, pulling her close.

"All I ever wanted was you." She was just glad she'd realized it in time.

"Back at you, baby."

Walter nosed his way between them, seeking attention, and they both leaned down to give it to him. Tara had a feeling this would be a permanent way of life from now on. And she couldn't ask for anything more.

* * * *

Also from 1001 Dark Nights and Carly Phillips, discover Dare to Tease, Sexy Love, Take the Bride, and His to Protect.

Sign up for the 1001 Dark Nights Newsletter
and be entered to win a Tiffany Key necklace.

There's a contest every month!

Go to www.1001DarkNights.com to subscribe.

**As a bonus, all subscribers can download
FIVE FREE exclusive books!**

Discover 1001 Dark Nights Collection Nine

DRAGON UNBOUND by Donna Grant
A Dragon Kings Novella

NOTHING BUT INK by Carrie Ann Ryan
A Montgomery Ink: Fort Collins Novella

THE MASTERMIND by Dylan Allen
A Rivers Wilde Novella

JUST ONE WISH by Carly Phillips
A Kingston Family Novella

BEHIND CLOSED DOORS by Skye Warren
A Rochester Novella

GOSSAMER IN THE DARKNESS by Kristen Ashley
A Fantasyland Novella

THE CLOSE-UP by Kennedy Ryan
A Hollywood Renaissance Novella

DELIGHTED by Lexi Blake
A Masters and Mercenaries Novella

THE GRAVESIDE BAR AND GRILL by Darynda Jones
A Charley Davidson Novella

THE ANTI-FAN AND THE IDOL by Rachel Van Dyken
A My Summer In Seoul Novella

A VAMPIRE'S KISS by Rebecca Zanetti
A Dark Protectors/Rebels Novella

CHARMED BY YOU by J. Kenner
A Stark Security Novella

HIDE AND SEEK by Laura Kaye
A Blasphemy Novella

DESCEND TO DARKNESS by Heather Graham
A Krewe of Hunters Novella

BOND OF PASSION by Larissa Ione
A Demonica Novella

JUST WHAT I NEEDED by Kylie Scott
A Stage Dive Novella

Also from Blue Box Press

THE BAIT by C.W. Gortner and M.J. Rose

THE FASHION ORPHANS by Randy Susan Meyers and M.J. Rose

TAKING THE LEAP by Kristen Ashley
A River Rain Novel

SAPPHIRE SUNSET by Christopher Rice writing as C. Travis Rice
A Sapphire Cove Novel

THE WAR OF TWO QUEENS by Jennifer L. Armentrout
A Blood and Ash Novel

THE MURDERS AT FLEAT HOUSE by Lucinda Riley

THE HEIST by C.W. Gortner and M.J. Rose

SAPPHIRE SPRING by Christopher Rice writing as C. Travis Rice
A Sapphire Cove Novel

MAKING THE MATCH by Kristen Ashley
A River Rain Novel

Discover More Carly Phillips

Dare to Tease: A Dare Nation Novella

She handles cocky jocks for a living, but her love life isn't as successful.

Brianne Prescott, publicist for Dare Nation Sports Agency, grew up the only girl with four brothers, three of whom are sports royalty. She's a pro not just at work but at being used by men who want access to her famous family. She's learned the hard way that everyone wants something from her, always.

He's her brother's best friend and the first man who sees her for who she really is.

When Dr. Hudson Northfield rescues Bri from a homeless man outside the clinic where he works, he really notices her for the first time. Soon she's accompanying him to New York for a family wedding, and despite her siblings' overprotective protests, they're falling in love.

But Hudson has a secret he can't reveal. If he wants access to a trust fund in his name, his father demands something in return. Hudson has to marry and provide an heir or his dream of opening a state-of-the-art health center will be destroyed. Suddenly the man who didn't need anything from her appears to be the biggest user of them all. Unless Hudson can convince her he can live without money but he can't live without her.

* * * *

Sexy Love: A Sexy Series Novella

Learning curves have never been so off-limits.

Professor Shane Warden is on the verge of getting tenure. He never thought he'd see the day, after a false accusation from a student years ago that nearly destroyed his career, and decimated his ability to trust. But the moment he walks into class and lays eyes on the seductive blonde with legs that go on forever and lips he immediately wants to kiss, he knows he's in trouble.

This time for real.

Single mom Amber Davis is finally living her dream of going back to college. In the ten years since she dropped out to have a baby--and recover from his father's death--it's been the goal that always felt just out of reach. Until now. But one look at her hot, sexy professor, and Amber is head over heels in lust. It doesn't take long before their attraction blazes out of control.

Neither of them can afford a forbidden affair.

Yet it's the one thing they are powerless to stop.

It will only take one hint of a rumor to destroy everything they've worked so hard to achieve... and in this case the rumors are true.

* * * *

Take the Bride: A Knight Brothers Novella

She used to be his. Now she's about to marry another man.
Will he let her go … or will he stand up and take the bride?

Ryder Hammond and Sierra Knight were high school sweethearts. Despite him being her brother's best friend, their relationship burned hot and fast…and ended with heartbreak and regrets.

Years later, she's at the altar, about to marry another man.

He's only there for closure, to finally put the past behind him.

But when the preacher asks if anyone has a reason the couple shouldn't wed, she turns around and her gaze locks on his.

Suddenly he's out of his seat.

Objecting.

Claiming.

And ultimately stealing the very pissed off bride and takes her to a secluded cabin.

He wants one week to convince her they're meant to be, to remind her of the fiery passion still burning between them.

When their time together is up, will she walk away and break *his* heart this time, or will he finally have the woman he's wanted all along?

* * * *

His to Protect: A Bodyguard Bad Boys/Masters and Mercenaries Novella

Talia Shaw has spent her adult life working as a scientist for a big pharmaceutical company. She's focused on saving lives, not living life. When her lab is broken into and it's clear someone is after the top secret formula she's working on, she turns to the one man she can trust. The same irresistible man she turned away years earlier because she was too young and naive to believe a sexy guy like Shane Landon could want *her.*

Shane Landon's bodyguard work for McKay-Taggart is the one thing that brings him satisfaction in his life. Relationships come in second to the job. Always. Then little brainiac Talia Shaw shows up in his backyard, frightened and on the run, and his world is turned upside down. And not just because she's found him naked in his outdoor shower, either.

With Talia's life in danger, Shane has to get her out of town and to her eccentric, hermit mentor who has the final piece of the formula she's been working on, while keeping her safe from the men who are after her. Guarding Talia's body certainly isn't any hardship, but he never expects to fall hard and fast for his best friend's little sister and the only woman who's ever really gotten under his skin.

Just One Spark

Kingston Family Book 4
By Carly Phillips
Now Available

Dash huddled in the corner of the overly large sofa in Xander's family room. While grumbling about too many people in his house, Xander had moved the band and Linc to a space with more sitting room. Status quo for his best-selling thriller author brother, whose books were made into hit movies. He liked a more solitary life.

Why Xander put up with Dash and his shit was beyond him. But Dash loved his older brother and always had. He'd pulled the same crap when they were kids, sleeping on the floor of Xander's bedroom until his mother bought a trundle bed so Dash was more comfortable.

Xander had grumbled then, too, Dash thought wryly. But if his life went to hell, Xander would be there and not say, *I told you so.* Not much, anyway.

Dash's cell rang, silencing everyone. He pulled out the phone from his pocket, glanced at the screen, and his heart began to pound harder in his chest.

"It's the lawyer," he said to his audience, men he trusted with his life. Men who'd been waiting to hear the news along with him. The band because of the publicity Dash had thrust on them, and along with his brothers, they cared.

Palms slick with sweat, Dash stood. He took the call, putting it on speaker because he didn't want to have to repeat the news if it was bad. "Peter, talk to me," he said to his attorney.

"Got the paternity results in my hand," the man said.

At that moment, Sasha walked in, Cassidy by her side. Because why shouldn't the woman who affected him on a soul-deep level witness his humiliation?

"Dash, you are *not* the father," Peter said without wasting time, and damned if Dash didn't drop to his knees in relief and disconnected the call.

"Fucking sounds like an episode of *Maury*," Axel said. "But you must be relieved. Congrats, man."

Linc and Xander surrounded him, and he rose to his feet, promising himself that, from this point on, his life would change. No more fucking groupies, no more being too wasted as an excuse.

He blinked, his gaze refocusing until he met Cassidy's damp stare, her pretty green eyes wet with unshed tears. She'd wrapped her arms around herself and his stomach cramped at the hurt he saw in her expression. Unable to deal with the pain he'd caused when he was still in the process of reconfiguring what he wanted out of life, he turned away.

And when he turned back to face Sasha and Cassidy, the women were nowhere to be found.

About Carly Phillips

Carly Phillips gives her readers Alphalicious heroes to swoon for and romance to set your heart on fire, and she loves everything about writing romance . She married her college sweetheart and lives in Purchase, NY along with her three crazy dogs: two wheaten terriers and a mutant Havanese, who are featured on her Facebook and Instagram. She has raised two incredible daughters who put up with having a mom as a romance author. Carly is the author of over fifty romances, and is a NY Times, Wall Street Journal, and USA Today Bestseller. She loves social media and interacting with her readers. Want to keep up with Carly? Sign up for her newsletter and receive TWO FREE books at www.carlyphillips.com.

Discover 1001 Dark Nights

COLLECTION ONE

FOREVER WICKED by Shayla Black ~ CRIMSON TWILIGHT by Heather Graham ~ CAPTURED IN SURRENDER by Liliana Hart ~ SILENT BITE: A SCANGUARDS WEDDING by Tina Folsom ~ DUNGEON GAMES by Lexi Blake ~ AZAGOTH by Larissa Ione ~ NEED YOU NOW by Lisa Renee Jones ~ SHOW ME, BABY by Cherise Sinclair~ ROPED IN by Lorelei James ~ TEMPTED BY MIDNIGHT by Lara Adrian ~ THE FLAME by Christopher Rice ~ CARESS OF DARKNESS by Julie Kenner

COLLECTION TWO

WICKED WOLF by Carrie Ann Ryan ~ WHEN IRISH EYES ARE HAUNTING by Heather Graham ~ EASY WITH YOU by Kristen Proby ~ MASTER OF FREEDOM by Cherise Sinclair ~ CARESS OF PLEASURE by Julie Kenner ~ ADORED by Lexi Blake ~ HADES by Larissa Ione ~ RAVAGED by Elisabeth Naughton ~ DREAM OF YOU by Jennifer L. Armentrout ~ STRIPPED DOWN by Lorelei James ~ RAGE/KILLIAN by Alexandra Ivy/Laura Wright ~ DRAGON KING by Donna Grant ~ PURE WICKED by Shayla Black ~ HARD AS STEEL by Laura Kaye ~ STROKE OF MIDNIGHT by Lara Adrian ~ ALL HALLOWS EVE by Heather Graham ~ KISS THE FLAME by Christopher Rice~ DARING HER LOVE by Melissa Foster ~ TEASED by Rebecca Zanetti ~ THE PROMISE OF SURRENDER by Liliana Hart

COLLECTION THREE

HIDDEN INK by Carrie Ann Ryan ~ BLOOD ON THE BAYOU by Heather Graham ~ SEARCHING FOR MINE by Jennifer Probst ~ DANCE OF DESIRE by Christopher Rice ~ ROUGH RHYTHM by Tessa Bailey ~ DEVOTED by Lexi Blake ~ Z by Larissa Ione ~ FALLING UNDER YOU by Laurelin Paige ~ EASY FOR KEEPS by Kristen Proby ~ UNCHAINED by Elisabeth Naughton ~ HARD TO SERVE by Laura Kaye ~ DRAGON FEVER by Donna Grant ~ KAYDEN/SIMON by Alexandra Ivy/Laura Wright ~ STRUNG UP by Lorelei James ~ MIDNIGHT UNTAMED by Lara Adrian ~

TRICKED by Rebecca Zanetti ~ DIRTY WICKED by Shayla Black ~ THE ONLY ONE by Lauren Blakely ~ SWEET SURRENDER by Liliana Hart

COLLECTION FOUR

ROCK CHICK REAWAKENING by Kristen Ashley ~ ADORING INK by Carrie Ann Ryan ~ SWEET RIVALRY by K. Bromberg ~ SHADE'S LADY by Joanna Wylde ~ RAZR by Larissa Ione ~ ARRANGED by Lexi Blake ~ TANGLED by Rebecca Zanetti ~ HOLD ME by J. Kenner ~ SOMEHOW, SOME WAY by Jennifer Probst ~ TOO CLOSE TO CALL by Tessa Bailey ~ HUNTED by Elisabeth Naughton ~ EYES ON YOU by Laura Kaye ~ BLADE by Alexandra Ivy/Laura Wright ~ DRAGON BURN by Donna Grant ~ TRIPPED OUT by Lorelei James ~ STUD FINDER by Lauren Blakely ~ MIDNIGHT UNLEASHED by Lara Adrian ~ HALLOW BE THE HAUNT by Heather Graham ~ DIRTY FILTHY FIX by Laurelin Paige ~ THE BED MATE by Kendall Ryan ~ NIGHT GAMES by CD Reiss ~ NO RESERVATIONS by Kristen Proby ~ DAWN OF SURRENDER by Liliana Hart

COLLECTION FIVE

BLAZE ERUPTING by Rebecca Zanetti ~ ROUGH RIDE by Kristen Ashley ~ HAWKYN by Larissa Ione ~ RIDE DIRTY by Laura Kaye ~ ROME'S CHANCE by Joanna Wylde ~ THE MARRIAGE ARRANGEMENT by Jennifer Probst ~ SURRENDER by Elisabeth Naughton ~ INKED NIGHTS by Carrie Ann Ryan ~ ENVY by Rachel Van Dyken ~ PROTECTED by Lexi Blake ~ THE PRINCE by Jennifer L. Armentrout ~ PLEASE ME by J. Kenner ~ WOUND TIGHT by Lorelei James ~ STRONG by Kylie Scott ~ DRAGON NIGHT by Donna Grant ~ TEMPTING BROOKE by Kristen Proby ~ HAUNTED BE THE HOLIDAYS by Heather Graham ~ CONTROL by K. Bromberg ~ HUNKY HEARTBREAKER by Kendall Ryan ~ THE DARKEST CAPTIVE by Gena Showalter

COLLECTION SIX

DRAGON CLAIMED by Donna Grant ~ ASHES TO INK by Carrie Ann Ryan ~ ENSNARED by Elisabeth Naughton ~ EVERMORE by

Corinne Michaels ~ VENGEANCE by Rebecca Zanetti ~ ELI'S TRIUMPH by Joanna Wylde ~ CIPHER by Larissa Ione ~ RESCUING MACIE by Susan Stoker ~ ENCHANTED by Lexi Blake ~ TAKE THE BRIDE by Carly Phillips ~ INDULGE ME by J. Kenner ~ THE KING by Jennifer L. Armentrout ~ QUIET MAN by Kristen Ashley ~ ABANDON by Rachel Van Dyken ~ THE OPEN DOOR by Laurelin Paige ~ CLOSER by Kylie Scott ~ SOMETHING JUST LIKE THIS by Jennifer Probst ~ BLOOD NIGHT by Heather Graham ~ TWIST OF FATE by Jill Shalvis ~ MORE THAN PLEASURE YOU by Shayla Black ~ WONDER WITH ME by Kristen Proby ~ THE DARKEST ASSASSIN by Gena Showalter

COLLECTION SEVEN

THE BISHOP by Skye Warren ~ TAKEN WITH YOU by Carrie Ann Ryan ~ DRAGON LOST by Donna Grant ~ SEXY LOVE by Carly Phillips ~ PROVOKE by Rachel Van Dyken ~ RAFE by Sawyer Bennett ~ THE NAUGHTY PRINCESS by Claire Contreras ~ THE GRAVEYARD SHIFT by Darynda Jones ~ CHARMED by Lexi Blake ~ SACRIFICE OF DARKNESS by Alexandra Ivy ~ THE QUEEN by Jen Armentrout ~ BEGIN AGAIN by Jennifer Probst ~ VIXEN by Rebecca Zanetti ~ SLASH by Laurelin Paige ~ THE DEAD HEAT OF SUMMER by Heather Graham ~ WILD FIRE by Kristen Ashley ~ MORE THAN PROTECT YOU by Shayla Black ~ LOVE SONG by Kylie Scott ~ CHERISH ME by J. Kenner ~ SHINE WITH ME by Kristen Proby

COLLECTION EIGHT

DRAGON REVEALED by Donna Grant ~ CAPTURED IN INK by Carrie Ann Ryan ~ SECURING JANE by Susan Stoker ~ WILD WIND by Kristen Ashley ~ DARE TO TEASE by Carly Phillips ~ VAMPIRE by Rebecca Zanetti ~ MAFIA KING by Rachel Van Dyken ~ THE GRAVEDIGGER'S SON by Darynda Jones ~ FINALE by Skye Warren ~ MEMORIES OF YOU by J. Kenner ~ SLAYED BY DARKNESS by Alexandra Ivy ~ TREASURED by Lexi Blake ~ THE DAREDEVIL by Dylan Allen ~ BOND OF DESTINY by Larissa Ione ~ MORE THAN POSSESS YOU by Shayla Black ~ HAUNTED HOUSE by Heather Graham ~ MAN FOR ME by Laurelin Paige ~

THE RHYTHM METHOD by Kylie Scott ~ JONAH BENNETT by Tijan ~ CHANGE WITH ME by Kristen Proby ~ THE DARKEST DESTINY by Gena Showalter

Discover Blue Box Press

TAME ME by J. Kenner ~ TEMPT ME by J. Kenner ~ DAMIEN by J. Kenner ~ TEASE ME by J. Kenner ~ REAPER by Larissa Ione ~ THE SURRENDER GATE by Christopher Rice ~ SERVICING THE TARGET by Cherise Sinclair ~ THE LAKE OF LEARNING by Steve Berry and M.J. Rose ~ THE MUSEUM OF MYSTERIES by Steve Berry and M.J. Rose ~ TEASE ME by J. Kenner ~ FROM BLOOD AND ASH by Jennifer L. Armentrout ~ QUEEN MOVE by Kennedy Ryan ~ THE HOUSE OF LONG AGO by Steve Berry and M.J. Rose ~ THE BUTTERFLY ROOM by Lucinda Riley ~ A KINGDOM OF FLESH AND FIRE by Jennifer L. Armentrout ~ THE LAST TIARA by M.J. Rose ~ THE CROWN OF GILDED BONES by Jennifer L. Armentrout ~ THE MISSING SISTER by Lucinda Riley ~ THE END OF FOREVER by Steve Berry and M.J. Rose ~ THE STEAL by C. W. Gortner and M.J. Rose ~ CHASING SERENITY by Kristen Ashley ~ A SHADOW IN THE EMBER by Jennifer L. Armentrout

On Behalf of 1001 Dark Nights,

Liz Berry, M.J. Rose, and Jillian Stein would like to thank ~

Steve Berry
Doug Scofield
Benjamin Stein
Kim Guidroz
Social Butterfly PR
Asha Hossain
Chris Graham
Chelle Olson
Kasi Alexander
Jessica Saunders
Dylan Stockton
Kate Boggs
Richard Blake
and Simon Lipskar

Made in the USA
Las Vegas, NV
27 March 2022